I0629476

Team Bangkok: Hearts on Ice

I. C. Denton, Jr.

Published by Tuk Tuk Press, 2022.

TEAM BANGKOK: HEARTS ON ICE

First edition. July 16, 2022.

Copyright © 2022 I. C. Denton, Jr..

ISBN: 979-8218065409

Written by I. C. Denton, Jr..

To my wife Judy, my heart, my love and companion for our marvelous journey through life.

1. Angela Arrives in Bangkok

Angela Tran shouldered her backpack, dodged her way through the passengers hauling their carry-ons from overhead bins, and burst through the jetway's tropical heat into the frigid air-conditioned Arrivals section of Suvarnabhumi airport. The gate agent welcomed her to Bangkok, pressing her palms together in the typical prayer-like greeting known in Thailand as a wai. Angela smiled and politely returned the wai. Once clear of the growing commotion, Angela grabbed her phone from her backpack and speed-dialed her father, the former Colonel Tran, USAF, now employed in Phnom Penh.

"We just landed in Bangkok, Dad, and I'm hyper-excited about what comes next."

"Welcome back to Thailand!" Colonel Tran said. "Your job will definitely be exciting."

"With the Khmer Rouge tribunals now close to ending, won't you be looking for new work yourself?" she asked.

"Actually, several opportunities have opened up, mildly exciting, nothing dangerous. We can talk more when you come to visit."

"I'll come as soon as I can. I'm on my burner phone."

"Good, can't be too careful. You know what to do with it."

"Yes. Got to find Milo. Love you, Dad."

Angela tossed her phone in a trash bin, moved through the Thai Citizens' entry, gathered her baggage from the carousel, and made her way past Customs.

The recently-completed Suvarnabhumi airport was already among the world's most efficient and photographed airports. A cause célèbre at its inception, the airport rose from a cobra swamp amid corruption scandals. Within its walls of steel and glass, moving walkways carried passengers through jungle gardens into a shopping mall atmosphere. Decorative touches of old Siam were everywhere.

Milo stood just beyond Customs, holding a welcome sign written in Thai Script. Milo was one of her father's former comrades-in-arms in the Air Force Intelligence base in the Ubon Ratchathani province near the Cambodian border. Many of the 'operators' still stayed in touch. Such longstanding connections had smoothed Angela's return to Thailand.

In her excitement, she assumed the familiarity of an old friendship: "Milo, you tattered old spy, oops, Boss. It's great to see you again. Thanks for meeting me. I can't wait to get started."

"Old and tattered, yes, but a spy, no more, Angela. Are you excited or just punch-drunk after a day-long flight?"

"I don't even know what day it is, Milo, and I haven't punched anyone since I was last here, but my nose for Thai food tells me I've arrived."

"Let's get out of here and head to your new digs. You have a ninth-floor serviced apartment above the fray with views up and down Soi Rangnam and across the city. Team Bangkok takes care of its people."

"I'll say! An escort from the airport to a furnished apartment with housekeeping. You'll spoil me."

"The team is excited to meet you. Bangkok is changing, of course, the new gradually displacing the old." They queued up for a taxi and gave their destination to the agent.

"Sorry you'll miss most of the scenery on the drive into Bangkok, but it's almost midnight," Milo remarked. "We are going to the PIP Tower," Milo told the driver, who looked taken aback by Milo's command of the Thai language.

"You speak good Thai for a *farang*," said the driver, clearly impressed.

"Thanks for the compliment."

Years earlier, when Milo started learning the Thai language at the Armed Forces Institute in Monterey, his instructor referred to him as a '*farang*'. Sensing a possible put-down, Milo bristled. Wary of annoying a former Green Beret, his instructor quickly explained, "No disrespect, Major; '*farang*' means 'foreigner' in Thai. You'll receive many compliments since you will speak the language well."

Angela's father, Colonel Tran, an American and a native Thai language speaker, had also trained at the Monterey Institute a decade before Milo and become a poster boy for excellence in the Cambodian language. He and Milo worked together and became fast friends as US Air Force Intelligence officers in Thailand during the Vietnam conflict and later during Pol Pot's Khmer Rouge genocide.

"And the young madam?" the driver queried in limited but most polite English.

"I was born in Ubon Ratchathani," Angela responded in the perfect five-tone Thai that *farangs* rarely master.

After the pleasantries, they left the airport behind. Reflections from brilliant digital billboards lighted the highway for several miles. Then, applying his flip-flop to the accelerator, the driver raced onto the freeway and urged the Corolla to about 150 km per hour, leaving the billboards quickly behind.

"It's a strange story, Milo, isn't it," said Angela, continuing their conversation in English for the sake of privacy. "With you Ubon intelligence guys, the past is always lurking somewhere in the present. Of course, I wouldn't be here if it weren't for your Ubon codebreaker, Dr. Stern. Of all things, Dr. Stern was on the review committee for my NIH grant application for mosquito research in Thailand!

"He somehow remembered me as 'little Angela', Colonel Tran's daughter. He said that the committee thought my malaria proposal was terrific, but...I knew what was coming next: A malaria vaccine, RTS.S, already under development and scheduled for pilot projects, so no need for my proposal. The committee wanted a laboratory team to surveil for emerging zoonotic pathogens, like SARS. 'We need to find them before they find us,' they explained.

"The rejection sent me straightaway into a funk, deflated, but Dr. Stern pumped me back up. He was a dear; he knew I had counted heavily on grant funding and didn't have a plan B. He also knew I wanted to work in Thailand.

"Dr. Stern said that I should talk to you about Team Bangkok. He described Team Bangkok as a covert investigative unit cloaked in intrigue. I could expect a whiff of adventure and some excitement after my years in training. And coincidentally, you were in Bethesda looking for a doctor, and he'd get us together.

"So, you and I met in that hole-in-the-wall restaurant, where you sat, a Singha beer on the table. You told me about Team Bangkok, and I was hooked.

"Stern was right. I'm ripe for some intrigue and adventure. When you described the idea of a covert UN operation looking out for possible heart transplantation tourism, I thought, 'Wooha, a big-time evil'! How did you get into that?"

"Long story, Angela. You know some of it. When the Ubon facility closed and you went to live with your aunt in Texas, Air Force intelligence created a new identity for your dad, shipped him to Phnom Penh, and inserted him into a panel of translators in the Khmer Rouge tribunals.

"I was discharged, too, but stayed in Thailand, moved to Bangkok, met my wife Chua, who runs our restaurant, and started an agency promoting Muay Thai fighters.

"All the while, the papers reported that kidney transplant prices were decreasing precipitously. So, I reasoned that falling kidney prices might prompt the existing kidney shops to upgrade their services to include hearts and told the UN so. They cogitated on that and produced the idea of Team Bangkok to investigate the possibility. So, I'm building the team now."

"By the way, I work with an old friend of yours, a former championship contender," said Milo.

"Don't tell me it's Kiet!"

"The one and only."

"Wow, Kiet and I go back to childhood in the villages. I took a year off from med school to work out in his Muay Thai training camp.

"Changing the subject," Angela went on, "when I was a kid, I imagined you operators going off post for grand adventures along the Cambodian border, but I gradually twigged to the dangers you faced on those missions."

"Things got challenging often enough," Milo replied. "But we were all young, hot-shot intelligence types, excitement junkies, and we did lots of stuff," Milo remarked, nostalgia creeping into his voice.

"Yes, I remember you, Mom, and Dad would leave for a few days and come back, jungle-dirty and charged up, high fiving. Do you recall a particular mission just before my sixteenth birthday when Mr. Smith from Bangkok went with you? I thought you might be going to Bangkok to get me a present. Do you recall that mission? "

"Ah, *the* Mr. Smith," said Milo, "our 'polyglot chameleon spy'. He blended in everywhere and adapted to any situation. A top agent. He had even developed a contact in the Khmer hierarchy...unbelievable."

"Yeah, Mom and Dad thought he was remarkable too."

"Anyway, I recall Mom picking up a package from the medical commissary as you four were leaving. I secretly hoped you were headed to the Bangkok PX to get me a birthday present. I was disappointed when you came back with big smiles and high-fives but no present. But isn't it interesting, though, that Pol Pot died on my sixteenth birthday?"

Mr. Smith did show up with a birthday present. It was a set of nesting dolls from Russia. He said, 'Happy Birthday, Angela,' and told me, 'These dolls are a metaphor for life since you can't shed your skin like a cobra. You'll figure it out in good time'.

"I admired how pretty the figures were, how neatly they stacked together. I turned to thank Mr. Smith, but he was gone.

"Who was Mom's package for? Where did you go?" Angela prodded.

"Angela, we did many big things, had lots of missions along the border, but were sworn to secrecy," said Milo, narrowing his eyes. "That one is secret too. We always documented our missions in detail. You can read them for yourself when they are made public. How about that?"

"That's years away, Milo. I've wondered about it forever, and I don't want to wait much longer for the details. When I was born, Dad pronounced my birthdate as auspicious. Dad's no oracle, but Pol Pot died on my sixteenth birthday! Probably an unlikely coincidence, but interesting nonetheless."

"Surely a coincidence, but propitious like your joining Team Bangkok!" said Milo, crossing his arms across his chest.

"Something else, Milo. Back then, your missions exposed you to some dangerous enemies with long memories who might someday emerge to harm you. Dad still keeps his eyes open even at this late date and has me carry a burner phone."

"We were all trained to keep our eyes open."

"Me too, Milo, me too."

The taxi delivered them to the PIP Tower, where a serviced apartment awaited Angela. Located in the Victory Monument area just off Soi Rangnam, the PIP Tower was a 17-story affair built in the fifties and has since been updated. A statue of an angel stood within a niche atop the hotel, keeping watch. Interesting to see in this Buddhist land.

"So, here we are at the end of your travels."

Angela's excitement had waned to restless exhaustion. She returned the greetings of the doorman and desk clerk with a native *Sawatdii" Kha"* and a polite wai and received wide smiles and wais in return. *Ahh, back home in the land of smiles!*

"Unpack and recover," said Milo. "I'll come by in the morning, and we'll walk over to our restaurant, eat breakfast, and start the day."

After they exchanged goodnights, Angela surveyed the hotel lobby, noting exits front and back, and went to her room. Her balcony overlooked the flickering nightlights of Bangkok and a pool below. *I hope things don't get too exciting. It's a long way to jump.*

As her excitement ebbed and Angela drifted off to sleep, she mused about how quickly she had bought into the whole Team Bangkok package. For one thing, working with a UN group appealed to her idealistic side. All the more so did the team's charge to investigate possible heart transplant tourism. Putting an end to such a monstrosity, if it existed, would be morally rewarding and, professionally, at least be tangentially medical.

2. Milo's Lament

Angela awakened refreshed and excited to get going. She stretched and luxuriated in bed for a couple of minutes and considered the coming day. After meeting with Milo for breakfast, Angela would go to the Thai Ministry of Medicine to discuss medical licensure and then drop by the MBK Shopping Center to purchase an electric fan to augment the air conditioning. Last night, hers had seemed finicky, turning off and on unpredictably. *Maybe the fan first and the license later. This is summer in Bangkok, after all.*

She showered, slipped into jeans and a top, and patted the framed picture of her parents. A momentary twinge of grief that her mother didn't live to see her practice in Thailand was offset by the cheering thought that she'd visit her dad soon.

She met Milo in the lobby. They headed down the alley to Soi Rangnam Street and turned right toward Milo and Chua's restaurant.

"When Chua and I opened our restaurant, Soi Rangnam was bursting with street life. But the culture of old Thailand is giving way to modernity at quite a loss," Milo said. Angela heard regret in his voice.

Angela gawked at the new high-end, duty-free mall rising three floors above a bright green lawn across the street. A giant sphere of the world seemed to rotate in a huge goblet of water outside the building. Cut glass inserts whose facets sparkled like jewels marked the capital cities across the globe.

"You are looking at the Royal Facets Complex, the RFC as they call themselves—everything goes by initials nowadays. Even Bangkok is BKK," said Milo.

"To me, that huge globe is the foremost symbol of change on Soi Rangnam. Customers fly in from those sparkling cities to shop duty-free for luxury items.

"So now, the RFC is a destination: People fly in, shop, and return without seeing Bangkok. They never step outside to spend money with

8

the street vendors and stalls. So sadly, along with its kiosks and street food, street life is losing its flavor."

Angela surveyed the line of expensive cars and luxe coaches moving through the RFC's long drive-up. "The shoppers do travel in style."

"Yes, it's part of the RFC's luxury package: expensive cars and luxe coaches bring shoppers from the airport, disgorge them, and return them for their flights home," Milo explained. "Shoppers never need to struggle with their purchases, for the RFC delivers them directly to their flights home.

"Shoppers who are exhausted can retire to the attached 5-star hotel. The operation is brilliant." Milo's tone held a grudging respect for the RFC's marketing genius and a distaste for its intrusion into his beloved neighborhood. The RFC signaled a new era for Soi Rangnam.

"I suppose it's all part of change, Milo. Travelers are creatures of the modern world. They drop in from 35,000 feet, book spiffy hotels, charter tours, and shop duty-free. They might not care about having a storybook experience of old times in foreign lands," said Angela.

Milo shrugged this comment off and continued like a doleful tour guide, "The building next to the RFC is the new Siam Surgicenter, standing where a grand old teak house stood when we came. Laborers showed up one day and set up camp with tents and an outdoor kitchen. They took that house down board by board by hand and hauled it away."

"Did they build it somewhere else? Maybe a piece of old Soi Rangnam is resurrected in the countryside."

"They probably sold the teak. It was worth a fortune five years ago. So, down went the teak house, and up rose this Siam Surgicenter with its landscaping and new sidewalks."

Walking along the worn and cracked sidewalks on their side of the street, Milo pointed out a short-stay hotel. "The short-stay hotels never change. They cater to quickie assignations. Customers park their cars behind canvas curtains, and spiral staircases lead them to bedrooms upstairs. You didn't know this when you were a child, but a significant part of Bangkok's tourism is the sex trade, mainly in several areas for *farangs*. So mostly locals patronize short-stays like this one."

Next to the short-stay, Angela spotted a deep, narrow beer bar with a handful of stools in the gloom populated by locals. Then came the first street vendor they'd seen. The elderly owner sat on a small red plastic chair beside a stand of stacked whole fruit. Milo stopped for a moment to tease her, and her face crinkled with a smile.

"She knows everything that happens on the street," Milo said as they walked on.

"You're saying she's a valuable source of local intelligence, you old spy."

Milo smiled at her. "Of course. Never underestimate the grandmothers."

Further down, in front of the new 7-Eleven, Milo exchanged greetings with the vendor of iced pineapple, mango, and dragon fruit from a cart. They laughed at some witticism.

"We send our customers across the street to this fine man for a fruit dessert," Milo said to Angela.

"I hear 7-Eleven has thoroughly colonized Thailand and much of Southeast Asia," Angela said.

"They've cornered the market on cell phone minutes in case you run out, and everyone gets their newspapers at one too." Milo stepped into the 7-Eleven and purchased today's *Siam Scimitar*.

Angela observed the myriad urban motorcycles—4-cycle ones and the new electrics—weaving among the cars along the street.

"This is where we cross. Remember to look right first. I don't want to tell your dad that his daughter was flattened on the first day in Bangkok."

"I'll bet you wouldn't object to a modern stoplight here," Angela quipped. Milo harrumphed, folded the paper, and waved it above his head to appeal for passage. Crossing, they navigated the relentless buzz of traffic to an open-air restaurant identified by a wooden sign as *Tii Baan Chua* in Thai Script, roughly *Chua's House* in English.

"Everybody calls it simply *Tii Baan*."

As they entered *Tii Baan*, Milo laid the newspaper on a table, and Chua came from the kitchen to meet them.

"Angela, this Chua, my wife. *Tii Bann* is her domain. Chua, this is Angela Tran, the grown daughter of my old boss, Colonel Tran. She's now a doctor and the newest member of Team Bangkok."

The women offered deep wais to one another. To Angela's eye, Chua was a child of Isaan. Her broad nose, high cheeks, and darker skin of that region were set off by her bright saffron and white chef's jacket.

"Milo said I would see old Siam in your brown eyes, Angela, and I do. Thailand is written in them."

Amid the greetings, Milo's eye caught the *Siam Scimitar's* front-page photo. Stunned, he exploded, "My God, look at this!"

They leaned over the shocking photo and glaring headline: "*Heart on ice! Heart spills from delivery box of sideswiped motorcycle.*"

"You warned the UN about something like this," Chua gasped.

Milo dropped his Thai and swore in soldiers' English, "Shi-it, son-of-a-bitch! You're right, but I considered it hypothetical." He repeatedly tapped the speed dial on his mobile, exploding each time, "Hearts are in play after all. Get a *Scimitar*. Frontpage story. Meeting in the lab tonight."

Just as he ended those calls, Milo's phone sounded the raucous squall of its Muay Thai ringside music.

"Shit. Something's come up over at the Lumpini office. I'll tend to that, then close down for the day." He handed the paper to Angela. "Wisut will be along in a few minutes. I'll be back as soon as I can. You'll meet the whole team later today. You'll have to put off your license application for another day."

3. Thirty-Second Pitch

Milo grabbed a tuk-tuk and headed to his office near the Lumpini Muay Thai arena, leaving Chua to show Angela around the restaurant. Angela learned that Chua was born in Khon Kaen, the main city in Northeastern Thailand, a land of Lao and Khmer heritage and geographically of the Mekong River watershed. Chua graduated from Khon Kaen University, then trained in the kitchens of the famous Siam Riverfront restaurant to become a credentialed Thai Chef. She and Milo met in that same restaurant. Milo had proceeded to flirt.

"He aimed those shocking eyes at me and chatted me up in his earnest Thai, which was quite nuanced for a *farang*, but his Thai etiquette needed polish. I saw to that. We married and opened *Tii Baan* back when Soi Rangnam was 'really Soi Rangnam' to use Milo's words."

By all appearances, *Tii Baan* was a typical open-front Thai restaurant-watering hole. Sixteen oscillating ceiling fans cooled customers and hummed just loudly enough to ensure privacy from table to table.

"We call the center two tables VIP tables. Preposterous, I know. That's where Milo's ex-pat friends solve the world's problems several nights a week."

Then Chua pointed out the menu, "It's almost infinite. We have all the local and regional dishes and serve up an occasional meat pie for our British friends. But we specialize in spicy Isaan dishes. Our customers come from all walks of life: Thai neighbors, embassy employees, tourists, and backpackers, too, starving for a burger—Milo's specialty—and a beer. They all love the place. In addition, some of Milo's personal friends—business leaders, the Bangkok police chief, and an army general—drop by occasionally for reasons other than their dining pleasure."

Angela listened as she looked around the restaurant. The front was open to the sidewalk and street. A few bottles of Johnnie Walker,

Jameson's Irish, and local Thai whisky sat on the short bar beneath a sign indicating that Singha, Chang, Leo, Tiger, Fosters, and Heineken were cold and ready. A Japanese stereo outfit winked red and green behind the bar. Angela spotted ceiling cameras aimed at the dining area, bar, kitchen doorway, and sidewalk.

"If the spirit moves him, Milo queues up his Eagles favorites, usually 'Hotel California', which he often sings himself," Chua said. "Customers either love it or hate it."

Toward the back-right corner, the amenities were basic. A small wall sign from a past business read 'Vet-Tech' and pointed an up-arrow to a dark, rickety staircase.

"What's up the stairs?" asked Angela.

"The stairs lead to a computer lab. No kidding. That's where the team generally meets."

"I'd never suspect it. I'm looking forward to seeing it."

A flimsy door on the right side of a hall beyond the stairway opened into a single-bowl WC, and further on stood a washbasin, by which hung a communal hand towel.

Yuck, is everybody using the same towel? Angela thought. There was also a paper towel dispenser. *That's better.* The kitchen door opened on the left, emitting spicy aromas and busy servers. Somehow the traffic got by, so long as everyone smiled.

"What a terrific restaurant," Angela remarked to Chua, "with a neighborhood atmosphere, great food and drink, and a cloistered redoubt upstairs for Team Bangkok. I got here just as things are starting to explode."

Chua excused herself, and Angela took a seat to street-watch and pondered her new path, when a man wearing a NY ball cap bounded in and sat down at Angela's table.

"Sorry to be late," the man said. "Just got off the Skytrain. So hearts are on the market now. What are the odds? I thought the whole idea was crazy. So you must be *the Angela* that Milo talks about. I'm Wisut. Good to meet you," he said, catching his breath…

"Angela said, "It did sound crazy. Sure, kidney transplant tourism has become endemic throughout Asia. But harvesting hearts for transplantation is incredible! I'd never have imagined a heart spilling from a motorcycle delivery box after a wreck! But the photo says hearts are in play. Yes, I'm *that* Angela. Good to meet you too, Wisut."

"The *Scimitar's* photo strikes me as preposterous as Santa coming down a chimney," said Wisut.

"Great analogy, Wisut, but Santa comes annually in the West. We can hope this heart thing is a unique event too, however doubtful. Speaking of unique, Milo told me some of your back story: advanced degrees at big schools, worked for a New York City bank, Chulalongkorn Professor of Artificial Intelligence, and on and on, including a startup collaborating with Team Bangkok. But you are a fairly young man."

Wisut tilted his head. "I hadn't expected you to look so Thai. A bit tall for a Thai woman, but the skin tone and mostly the eyes—the Khmer look about them—and the hair, definitely Thai features," said Wisut without pause. "Yes, I was an IT guy at a New York City bank, and now I'm a professor of computer science. Here's the 30-second pitch:

"What do you do after finishing your Ph.D. at MIT in your early twenties? My Mom said I needed socializing. New York banks were recruiting, so I signed up, got an apartment in Manhattan, socialized, followed the Yankees, and went to work. My job was to create AI algorithms that would addict customers based on their purchasing history. However, it seemed unfair to me and un-Buddhist, and the work was boring. I was making lots of money, but I was losing my fastball."

"Nice sports analogy."

"So, when Chulalongkorn University announced a search for a Computer Science chair, I submitted my name and got the nod right away, possibly owing to Thai chauvinism. I am a Thai native and, in all modesty, a home-grown math prodigy. So now I'm back in the game: Chulalongkorn University professor of computer science and founder of an AI company."

"It certainly sounds like you are the man for the job!" Angela said. "I'm a Thai native, too. A midwife delivered me in the village clinic rather than on the Air Force base where Mom and Dad worked. But with American parents, I'm an American, too. Two languages, two cultures. Wahoo!"

"Our cognitive neuroscientist, Malcolm Bren, is an American. He's working to connect our inner and outer worlds with computer-brain interface models. He also consults with the philosophy department on the hard problems of consciousness and self. Don't ask.

"I brought Yasuhiro into the department too. He's an art prodigy and world-famous computer game auteur. I've built intelligent bots for his games. We believe they have translational applications for robotics. You'll meet Yasuhiro after he gets back from his trek."

"His trek? That's interesting."

"Yes. Yasuhiro's training in an elephant camp right now. Next month he and a mahout will trek along some old smuggling trails through Burma and Laos. Yasuhiro wants to imbue the animatronic characters in his games with genuine sensibilities, starting with elephants."

"What eclectic topics," interjected Angela, allowing Wisut to catch his breath. "Do you think Yasuhiro will author a computer game about heart smuggling?"

"There's a good chance he may do just that after today's *Scimitar* photo. So here I am, hunting for heart smugglers, whom I thought were imaginary, but aren't. It's weird. One question: As a former Texan, how do cobras compare to rattlesnakes?"

"Fun topic, especially when comparing their forked tongues and fangs with the human ilk. And my question to you is, why does Team Bangkok need an AI operation with a prodigy such as yourself already on board?"

4. Team Gathering

Chua lowered the metal security shutter to the sidewalk in preparation for the afternoon meeting. Everyone would meet Angela and rant about the *Siam Scimitar's* stunning front-page photo.

Chua, Wisut, and Angela ascended the dark stairs behind the Vet-Tech sign to a metal landing and a steel door. A touchpad triggered the door open into an immaculate, air-conditioned room the same size as the restaurant below. Computers with glowing displays, keyboards, and sophisticated electronics resided on lab tables. Melamine laminated walls bathed in blue light displayed the computer experts' scribblings and mathematical symbols. The floor was soundproof, and the windows were blacked out. The restaurant customers would never suspect a computer laboratory lurked just above their heads.

"Welcome to the lab," Wisut said. Slightly annoyed faces rose above computer screens at the intrusion, but the programmers politely waied. Wisut introduced them as his postdocs. An interactive whiteboard faced the end of a long conference table.

Having raced up the stairs, Milo arrived out of breath and waied to everyone, forcing the postdocs' hands again from their keyboards. Fidgeting with his phone and shifting from foot to foot, he smiled and suggested they show Angela outside. He jostled another door open onto a landing with a staircase connecting it to the courtyard behind *Tii Baan*.

"I thought Kiet would already be here. I wonder if Dr. Dow is back from the hospital?"

As they descended the stairs, Angela noted a Spirit House poised upon a pillar in a setting of bamboo and broad-leaf succulents in the back left corner of the courtyard below. A Brahmin priest had designated its location as favorable to local guardian spirits who dwelled inside. A charging station for electric vehicles stood along the back fence. A sentinel guardhouse that permitted only motorcycles, tuk-tuks, bicycles, and foot traffic opened in the back right corner. Next to it stood a renovated short-stay hotel with new canvas curtains across its three garages, squaring the courtyard.

"Dow and Alec use the units above the garages for their free clinic," Milo explained. Alec is back in England at the moment. They planned it for prostitutes, always prone to illness and injury, their children, and poor people. They installed an elevator for disabled patients and a spiral staircase for others," Milo explained and added, "Dow should be here in a minute."

"Kiet keeps his personal gym in the middle garage below the clinic. He works out there and runs in the Peace Park just down the street. His workshop is in the last garage."

"That's the Kiet I know," Angela said. "I can't wait to see him again. When we were children, Kiet relieved a cobra of its head with a length of bamboo as it rose up and flared at me. Even at that early age, a serious Buddhist, Kiet was stricken by killing this living creature and vowed to make merit. I thought saving my life would have made merit enough."

"Has the story grown over the years by any chance?"

"It has not. Milo, you of all people know Kiet's abilities."

"True, not as a cobra fighter, but as a Muay fighter. Kiet's parents signed him up early with a trainer. Unfortunately, in his late teens, Kiet suffered a career-ending injury in the national championship match. Of course, Muay fighters never like to see another fighter injured, but a few challengers weren't sorry to see Kiet leave the ring."

An electric tuk-tuk whooshed past the guardhouse into the courtyard, and Kiet climbed out. He waied politely to everyone, winked at Angela, and suddenly unleashed a spinning Muay Thai attack on her.

Pivoting on his right foot, Kiet aimed his left foot at Angela's chin, which she dodged, and, following his momentum, Kiet spun a croc-tail kick with his right heel toward Angela's jaw. Though caught by surprise,

Angela dodged again and applied a roundhouse kick of her own behind Kiet's left knee. His leg collapsed, and Kiet spun to the ground.

"And hello to you, too, old friend!" Angela said, laughing. "You are still the toughest Muay I know despite your injury. I still watch your old fights on YouTube. And I stay in shape too, as you probably noticed." Angela offered him a hand. He took it and hauled himself up. "I am so happy to see you in person again."

"Great to see you too, Angela, my favorite *farang* Muay. You've obviously kept your technique," Kiet grinned. His solid build looked as if hewn from Lao teak. His muscles lay like lengths of jungle vine beneath polished golden skin.

After his retirement, Kiet and a former female Muay Thai, a champion herself, started a training camp near Phuket alongside the Andaman Sea. Their professional reputations brought fame to the camp.

Burned out from clinical pressures, Angela took a year off to train in Kiet's camp after her internship. He let her break into the camp's waiting list because of their close friendship but assigned a no-nonsense coach for real Muay Thai training.

Learning the sport was a daily exercise in bruising exhaustion—practicing the basic postures and strikes, running in sand, shadow boxing, sit-ups and pushups, punching and kicking and kneeing the heavy bag, sparring to exhaustion as unsparing coaches gazed on, and endlessly picking herself up from the mat, until unable to continue. Sleeping at night and training again every morning was the rule. Full-time training was an experience of physical misery and mental grit like she had never known. Finally donning the robes of a combatant, Angela fought an amateur match on the women's circuit. She left the camp without medals but with the physical rewards of strength, speed, heightened agility, and the toughness of mind and heart of a Muay Thai fighter.

"I was always Kiet's great fan," Milo said. "After becoming friends, Kiet's trainer allowed me to watch Kiet work out. Then, after two years of negotiations and his unfortunate injury, Kiet joined me in the fighter recruitment-and-sponsoring business. Then came Team Bangkok's UN contract, and Kiet fit in perfectly."

Dr. Dow came down from her clinic and joined them as the sun sank westward. Milo proceeded with the introductions. "Khun Dr. Dow, this is Dr. Angela; Angela, Dow," Milo said, introducing the two. "Angela, Dow is Cambodian."

"Yes, and one of the lucky ones," Dow said. "I made it into Thailand just in time. Two million others perished in the Khmer Rouge genocide. I worked as a doctor in Khao I Dang, the first of many refugee camps that sprang up in short order. So many sick and starving survivors crossed the border that I stopped counting."

"I grew up near that border but had no notion of the atrocities you saw," Angela said.

"It was my introduction to true suffering," Dow said. "A few years after the war, I visited Phnom Penh and learned that the Khmer Rouge had turned my old high school into Security Prison 21. My old school, where thousands were tortured and killed, serves as the Tuol Sieng Genocide Museum. It's no longer a school for kids, but a Government-sponsored tourist destination that educates visitors about the reality of evil."

Angela said, "I only had an inkling of the evil. But up close and personal, it must have been horrible for you."

"Yes, we'll have to talk more about the Khmer Rouge and the Tribunals sometime. Unfortunately, the Tribunal has convicted only three senior leaders of crimes against humanity—including Duch, the psychopath who ran Tuol Sieng. Unfortunately, hundreds of KR murderers still survive, many living here in Thailand. Milo said he and your dad worked the Cambodian border during the genocide years—they saw it all—and that your father now translates at the

Khmer Rouge tribunals. The tribunals are finally plodding toward a disappointing end. Your dad still lives in Phnom Penh, right?"

"Yes," Angela replied. "As a recently-retired simultaneous translator at the tribunals, not as Colonel Tran, the former intelligence officer."

Dow's small stature belied the size of her heart. She had the darkest of dark eyes, blue-black hair, and the sweetest of smiles. Memories had forced tears from her eyes, and she appeared younger than middle age. She paused to gather herself, raised her chin, and said, "Alec and I work at City-1 Hospital. He's in the microbiology lab, and I'm in internal medicine."

"I heard that the King and his family are treated there," Angela said, "and I look forward to seeing City-1. But aren't there several other closer hospitals?"

"Oh yes, but City-1 was the most important hospital in Bangkok when we moved here. Over the past few years, other hospitals have fallen on tough times, but not City-1," Dow said. "Three have gone broke, and one of them was purchased by investors. That's the defunct hospital on Ratchathewi road, near here. Milo told you that patients with healed flank incisions—typical for kidney donations—have been showing up in our clinic, right? We believe the Surgicenter is buying kidneys, and our patients are selling."

"Are you investigating organ trafficking at City-1?" Angela asked.

"No, City-1 is not in the game," Milo broke in. However, we know the Surgicenter is in the kidney tourism business," he said. "But, like I said, kidneys are here to stay. We just have to be sure the Surgicenter isn't getting into hearts. Kiet, tell Angela about your projects."

"I have two projects, Angela. I converted my tuk-tuk into an electric one and installed a stereo system that coordinates tuk-tuk sounds with changing speed, which is very cool. I've also outfitted our drone with a pocket-sized jet engine like the ones for hobbyist model airplanes. It turns a generator to charge the batteries but adds no propulsion. I added a GPS and an infra-red camera for heat detection and night flight. It's extremely maneuverable and ideal for quiet surveillance. Wisut's postdocs are developing a swarm algorithm so that many drones can fly together like a murmuration of blackbirds."

Milo smiled, "Kiet is on a local drone racing team that has competed in Australia and China. They've won a few Baht in the competitions, but the guys are keeping their day jobs."

Kiet said, "So, Angela, did you expect a photo of a stolen heart on your first day back?"

"I expected exciting things but never imagined that."

Kiet agreed, "Milo got it right. Hearts are in play."

Milo spoke up, "It's our reality now. I'm getting angry again."

"I had doubted it, too," Wisut said. "But working with quantum mechanics, I can believe almost anything."

"I suppose this is the excitement that Dad and Dr. Stern predicted," said Angela.

"It's probably just beginning, Angela, Milo said. So, for now, I propose we have a beer and a quick dinner, go home and let our minds wander. We'll move tonight's meeting until tomorrow and figure out our next steps." Milo welcomed Angela to the team once again and wished everyone sweet dreams.

5. Nightmares

It was clear that nobody had had sweet dreams as the team moped into the computer lab the next day. They took seats at the conference table and hovered appreciatively over cups of coffee and tea from the kitchen. "Thank goodness for Chua," someone mumbled. An image of yesterday's front page dominated the whiteboard and commanded everyone's attention.

"You guys look as wrung-out as I feel," said Milo. "Nightmares wouldn't stop. The worst was when the heart started beating and shimmied off the crushed ice."

"A faraway voice from an empty chest pleading for life was my worst," Angela said.

"Mine was hearing the heart's sigh at its agonal quiver," said Kiet. "And looking at the whiteboard today doesn't help. The photo is revolting, and it takes up most of the front page. What's below the fold?"

"So, the photo is already speaking to us in our nightmares. That's terrific!"

"You've lost me, Milo," said Dow, who hadn't left for the hospital.

"I mean we don't understand the photo yet, but subconsciously we're trying to make sense of it in our dreams."

"Don't let this get too weird, Milo," Kiet joked.

"Stay with me, Kiet. I'm suggesting we look beneath the surface. Let's scour the photo for details and consciously analyze them.

"For example, our special forces trainers taught us to look for the tank in the trees, see the branch that's an AK-47, smell smoke or privies, and notice when the birds stop singing. So, let's hear what our sixth sense tells us."

Someone at the table said, "I get it. The shock of yesterday's photo so distracted us that we couldn't appraise it dispassionately. So today, we need to cool off, examine it calmly, and try to uncover its message, right?"

"It's like watching horror porn," Kiet said, and everybody nodded.

"Kiet's right about looking below the fold, too. I took a look. There are several unrelated articles there," said Wisut. "Massacres in Burma are still going on, people being beaten bloody, monks in revolt, but no photos of the violence. Umm...Aung San Suu Kyi's under house arrest again. The US has imposed gem sanctions that aren't starving the junta's finances yet, but gem prices will skyrocket. Oh, and this is interesting. An elderly woman and her attendant have overstayed their visas and disappeared." He scanned further. "Says she's in bad health."

"Wisut, do you suspect the heart was meant for her?" Angela asked.

"Could be," said Dow, pouring herself another cup of coffee. "This isn't just any heart. Its great vessels—the aorta and the venae cavae—appear surgically excised and prepped for transplantation."

"So, summing it up, we have a delivery-motorbike accident. Its cargo box has broken apart and spilled a river of crushed ice, and on that ice lies a surgically excised human heart," Milo said.

"Brrr," Milo shivered. "There are a few strands of wire and some surgical tubing running from a small metal box. Were those connected to the heart before impact? Any ideas? Could that box be a pacemaker or a mini heart pump?"

"Brilliant, Milo. Either might be necessary, but oxygen is definitely vital. However, I've never seen a pump oxygenator that small. Even pediatric ones aren't that small," Angela said. "That implies some serious engineering."

Wisut added, "So, we are talking advanced technical expertise. The police sent the device to the Department of Engineering at Chulalongkorn University to examine it. I'll call and get their take on it."

"My eyes always go to the fractured tibia poking through the rider's skin above his flop-flop," said Kiet. He shook his head and looked away. "Why was he side-swiped by a hit-and-run driver in broad daylight doesn't make sense. What are the odds?"

"Good question, Kiet," Milo said.

"And a photographer *just happened* to be at the crash site?" Dow said doubtfully.

Milo paused for a swallow of hot coffee. "We'll follow those threads."

"The heart looks young and healthy to me, reddish-purple, suggesting recent excision. It could have had a few final quivers like Kiet dreamed. It's nonviable now, of course," Dow said.

"How long can a heart survive outside a body?" Wisut asked.

"Without oxygen, hardly more than six minutes—the heart's so-called 'golden period' of viability. When a heart is stopped for surgical repair," Angela continued, "a heart-lung machine takes over, pumping oxygenated blood into the patient's circulation and preserving the heart's viability."

"A mini pump-oxygenator would solve the viability problem, but there are still the issues of compatibility and availability for heart transplantation," Dow said.

"Availability is an enormous problem everywhere," Angela said. "Most countries keep a national database of potential recipients and their compatibility factors, body sizes, and travel times between hospitals. A compatible recipient is identified in the database when a heart becomes available after an accident or medical death. Medical personnel speed the donor heart to the hospital, often by air. The recipient is usually waiting in the OR. So, in a legitimate scenario, an available heart comes first, and then a compatible recipient is identified."

Angela continued, "But for a black-market heart transplant scenario, I envision a tourist arriving first, tested for compatibility, and a suitable donor selected from a database. Almost same-day service, you might say."

Dow said, "So, to be clear, a commercial heart business must have an immediate source of compatible hearts. Unlike a blood bank, you can't keep an inventory of hearts on a shelf. A reliable supply requires a community of living donors, which means—"

"It means a captive community, probably a vulnerable ethnic community in a country opaque to outside scrutiny," said Angela, completing Dow's surmise. "The Rohingya and other ethnic minorities in Burma or the Chinese Uyghurs, or Falun Gongs fit that bill, and prisoners too, for that matter."

"China and Burma would both work," Wisut said. "However, China is playing nice on the international stage and guards its reputation carefully. Kidney transplantation is not a criminal offense in China, and, in fact, it brings in a billion dollars annually. So why jeopardize their reputation by selling hearts?

"However, Burma stays quietly out of sight and needs the trade. Whatever the case, the UN is worried about captive communities and cultural genocide. So, my money is on Burma."

"Mine, too," said Milo, "Burma is small and opaque to journalists and human-rights monitors. They've been at smuggling for centuries and have well-oiled networks for moving gems, drugs, teak, whatever, and hearts could fit right in."

"But Burma's technology is backward. So, they would have to import mini pump-oxygenators," said Angela.

"Let's assume the hearts come from Burma, the likely source being from captive Rohingya people or another ethnic minority," said Milo.

"It seems that harvesters would want to keep their operations secret. We learned about this heart because of an apparent accident. How many others have gone undetected?" Dow wondered. "That's frightening. I foresee universal revulsion and outcries to shut down heart tourism."

"Yes, if the repercussions from a single heart spilling from a delivery box are bad, just wait until dead bodies start showing up post-op," said Kiet. "How could a real heart surgeon get involved in something this depraved?"

"Almost unimaginable to me," said Angela. "No way could you persuade real heart surgeons to work in a murderous transplant enterprise."

"Good point," said Milo, "How many surgeons would you need? Couldn't one psychopath with a fast plane handle both ends of the process? I mean, harvest the heart at site A and fly the heart to site B and transplant it?"

"A hard day's work," Angela said. "But possible with one surgeon. Still, two sophisticated surgical facilities would be necessary, perhaps in a general hospital with a cardiac service at the harvesting end and a smaller sophisticated surgical suite at our end. We should try to find one here."

"So, we've considered availability, suitability, and ability. What about the financial feasibility of such an enterprise?" Wisut said. "What business plan would support a venture of this magnitude? Who would provide the set-up costs and ongoing expenditures? I'm thinking that whoever bankrolls this has smuggling expertise and substantial capital."

"So, we need to look for financial footprints and physical sites capable of doing the surgery," said Milo.

"I'm struck by what Wisut said earlier about the ill, elderly tourist who overstayed her visa," Kiet said. "Could she be the person who purchased the heart in the photo? Find her, and we might find the transplant facility."

"Good point," said Milo. "Somewhere in Bangkok may lie a bedridden patient with a failing heart and diminishing hope, waiting for a murdered person's heart that fell out of a delivery box and will never arrive."

"We should keep an eye on the crematoria in Bangkok," Dow said.

The reality of crematoria stunned the team. Dow looked even more serious. Kiet sat on his heels, looking vaguely toward the wall. Angela looked like she had already seen too many post-op deaths. Milo looked like he'd enjoy an early afternoon glass of wine or something stronger.

6. True Heartache

The team was mentally exhausted and emotionally drained the next morning, and by lunchtime, they required respite from the foul images and their horrible implications. So, they bolted from the lab for lunch and descended upon the closest food stall, where they settled themselves on small plastic stools around a makeshift table and gulped glasses of cold Thai tea. The cook laid out the day's offerings of green papaya salad, drunken noodles, chicken satays, and sweet green curry. Then, having devoured their lunches, they walked to the iced-fruit wagon in front of the 7-Eleven for chilled pineapple, watermelon, mango, and papaya skewers.

"I needed that," said Milo, opening the afternoon session. "Let's try to stay alert and move on. Considering everything we've discussed, the mechanics of their likely supply chain are fairly straightforward. They select a 'donor' with a compatible heart from a database at point A, excise that person's heart, ship it to point B—presumably in Bangkok—and transplant it into a paying recipient. It's an operating room-to-operating room affair. Easy to say, but the details are complex at points along the way. Dow, your thoughts?"

"That's our presumption. So, again, when a heart transplant patient arrives in Bangkok, the database—presumably in Burma—is tapped for a suitable, immediately-available compatible 'donor' whose heart will be harvested, packaged up, and shipped to Bangkok for transplant the same day."

"Whoa," said Kiet. "Harvested sounds like a clinical euphemism for cutting out a beating heart. We're not talking about mangos. Makes me want to vomit."

"It is revolting," said Dow. "To me, casual murder for a commercial heart transplant seems as evil as the Khmer Rouges' ideological killings of innocents. Murder's murder, but harvesting a human heart for business purposes seems worse."

"My opinion too, Dow," said Milo. "That being said, shipping a heart should be no problem for professional smugglers."

"I doubt they'll use motorbikes at point B again," joked Kiet.

"Yeah, not even to solve the last-mile problem, Kiet. The last mile is often a problem but hardly the thorniest. Add the need for skilled surgical-technical personnel at both ends," concluded Milo.

"With all that in mind," Angela asked, "why even go into the heart business? Why not just settle for kidney transplantation? The kidney business is profitable, quietly overlooked by authorities, and nobody gets hurt nowadays. It's a piece of cake in today's market."

Wisut responded, "It's the old supply-demand axiom, of course. Heart patients face different threats than kidney patients do. Even with failed kidneys, patients can live for years on dialysis. However, there's no way to keep end-stage hearts beating, so these patients unavoidably face death. And therefore, are willing to pay huge prices for transplanting a fresh one."

Angela added, "So, with thousands of heart patients awaiting certain death and donor hearts being in short supply, this is high-value stuff."

"High-value stuff for sure," Wisut confirmed. "I'll bet a black-market transplant would bring $1.5 million US. Big profits, yes, but something else nags at me: managing the expenses—getting over the hump—while keeping everything secret as the business grows? I haven't figured that one out even with my banker's hat on. So, we may be overlooking something."

"Let's stay out of that rabbit hole for now, Wisut," Milo cautioned. "Let's keep our eyes open and keep turning over stones. Clues won't just fall into our laps."

"Isn't it time for Angela to get her bike?" asked Kiet, yawning.

"That's the non sequitur of the day, Kiet," Milo said. "But Angela needs to get her medical license first. First the license, then the bike. Then we'll check out our neighbors at the Surgicenter.

"Tomorrow's a big day."

7. An Electric Day

After the evening of macabre thought experiments, Angela was glad to have something less burdensome to think about the next morning. *Today, I'll apply for my medical license, get an electric motorcycle, and see Bangkok with Kiet.* She also needed to recharge her mobile's minutes at the 7-Eleven.

Angela showered and slipped into her business outfit: a skirt to her knees, grey two-button blazer, white dress shirt, neck open for a necklace to match her bracelet. She slipped on low-heel, closed-toe shoes. *No flip-flops today.* She patted her parents' picture, gathered her medical papers, regulated the AC, and wondered if she had passed the online Thai medical examinations she had taken in the US. *But, of course, I did.*

After breakfast, she stepped from the lobby into a bright, warm day.

"She summoned a taxi and gave directions to the driver. She smiled to herself, "What a wonderful day! I'll be a Thai physician with a new bike!"

When Angela arrived at the Medical Council's offices, the Minister of Health personally welcomed her. "*Sawatdii Kha*, Khun Angela, I'm Noi."

Angela responded, "*Sawatdii Kha*, Khun Doctor Noi." They exchanged polite, slightly formal, high wais, bypassed the reception desk, and walked directly to Dr. Noi's office.

Dr. Noi sifted through Angela's papers. "First of all, you passed the online examinations with high numbers. Congratulations! Were the exams hard for you in Thai?"

"No, Khun Noi. I'm about as Thai as they come. I was born here in a village near Ubon Ratchathani. My parents were Air Force officers. I went to school in Ubon with all the local kids instead of on the base until I was sixteen," Angela continued.

"After my mother died, I moved to South Texas to live with Mom's twin sister. I worked my way through school in the US doing Thai translations for various universities and government agencies. So, I kept my Thai."

"I want to keep my English, too, but I get so little practice. Is it okay if we speak English?" said Noi.

"Wonderful. Just hearing that question tells me your English is excellent."

"I see your mother was a doctor, too," Noi said. "Did she inspire you to be a doctor?"

"Yes, she did, Khun Noi. After Mom finished rounds at the base, she usually rounded in the nearby villages. I'd go with her whenever I could. Sometimes she consulted with the local shamans. Western medicine could treat ninety percent of patients' illnesses, but many difficult medical conditions surrendered only to shamans' invocations to healing spirits. That often gave Mom goosebumps—me too."

"We doctors get it right most of the time, but some things are beyond us," said Noi. "Incidentally, I spent time in Texas, too, on a Thailand Government scholarship. It carried me through the first two years of med school at UT. I finished the final two in med school in Bangkok at Mahidol University."

Dr. Noi turned another page in Angela's dossier. "It says here that your mother died of malaria."

"My goodness, you must have left the University of Texas medical school before I started. And, yes, Mom died of cerebral malaria," Angela continued. "Malaria was an endemic enemy — it still is. Mom fought it fiercely from village to village with education and meds until the parasites gradually developed resistance. I plan to do the same but with today's medications. We are likely to see a vaccine for Malaria in our lifetimes, far too late to save Mom.

"One day on village rounds, Mom stopped and stared into space, cried out, fell to the forest floor, and convulsed. I held her close and cried, 'somebody help.' The village shaman appeared, took my hand, and conjured words that quieted Mom's fatal seizure.

"Then he looked into my eyes, wiped my cheeks, and murmured something in a strange language. I don't know what he said or why it worked, but his words calmed me. He told me to grieve with pride, but never self-pity, for Mom's life had completed her cycle. Her spirit would live in me now. I knew then that I'd be a doctor.

"I apologize, Dr. Noi. I didn't mean to be so sentimental."

Dr. Noi took her hand and said, "Not at all, Dr. Tran. That was your Thai self speaking, not your Western one. I understand and think that experience will serve you well upcountry. And please call me Noi."

"Thank you, Noi, and please call me Angela. I'm of two minds and two cultures with no conflicts between spirits and science. I admire how shamans work without using our scientific tools. They understand things that we don't."

"I do too. That's an unambiguous answer to the question that modern Thai doctors often have to answer. I'll remember it."

Dr. Noi flipped through Angela's papers a final time. "I see you live in the PIP Tower in the Victory Monument area. That's near the Siam Surgicenter, isn't it?"

"Yes, it is close by, and I'm considering applying for temporary staff privileges there. Anything I should know about it?"

"I'm an administrator, but I try to keep my finger on Bangkok's medical pulse. The Surgicenter's specialty practice is a recent concept here. Our doctors fear it will 'skim the cream' and threaten their practices."

"It was the same in the US early on," Angela responded, "but specialists and patients like the surgical centers. However, it's been creative destruction for general hospital surgery departments with arguments pro and con."

"Dr. Julian and Dr. Hu are the only two surgeons on the Surgicenter staff," Noi continued. "They like the specialty concept, but how they got together is a mystery to me. Dr. Julian graduated from Chulalongkorn Medical University in Bangkok. Dr. Hu, a native Thai with Chinese ancestry, trained in surgery in Beijing.

"Hu's family lives upcountry near the Golden Triangle. They immigrated decades ago from the Guangdong area in China, and some of the older generation folks still speak a Chinese dialect. After training in Beijing, Hu's fluent in Mandarin.

"But it does seem unusual that Doctor Hu arrived, fresh out of training, knowing nobody in the Bangkok medical community, and setting up in a private specialty hospital. It's as if the hospital was built with him in mind. I'll be interested to hear your thoughts if you join the staff," Noi concluded.

"Yes, it is strange to find surgical talent practicing on the periphery of the medical community," Angela said, knowing that she couldn't reveal Team Bangkok's plans for her in that facility.

"Well, I'm glad you successfully managed the annoying exam requirements," Noi said. "Let me be the first to say, 'Welcome to Medicine in Thailand'! They are printing up your license as we speak. I'm sure we'll be seeing each other again."

"I do hope so." As Angela prepared to leave, they exchanged wais as friends.

I really like Dr. Noi, Angela thought. Returning to her apartment, she changed clothes and waited for Kiet beneath the PIP's porte-cochere. She didn't hear his electric motorcycle whisper up. Startled, she turned, took a breath, and asked, "Will my bike be this quiet?"

"Let's get one and find out. Hop on." As they whirred out onto Soi Rangnam, Angela sat pillion on the motorcycle, her hair streaming back.

Wind in my face again, she thought. She wondered if Kiet recalled their bike trip to Surin for the elephant festival as kids. A cloud of blue smoke from their old two-stroke bikes had followed them. *And here I am now, perched on the back of Kiet's electric motorcycle, zipping through Bangkok as a newly minted Thai physician. Quite a long way from elephants!*

Angela's dreamy state dissipated when Kiet drew up to a motorbike storefront and parked. Kiet knew a lot about motorcycles, and many of the salespeople remembered Kiet's Muay Thai bouts at Lumpini Stadium.

So, the salespeople greeted Kiet and Angela with brilliant smiles and respectful wais as the two surveyed the display of motorcycles.

"They all look so much alike," she said.

"Yes, they do," Kiet said, "because there are so few models now. But electric motorcycles are the future, and I see some terrific ones lined up along the sidewalk here."

The salesman told Angela about the popular brands in infinite detail and gave his personal recommendations, not once mentioning prices.

He said, "Their instant acceleration is either thrilling or scary, depending on the driver's tolerance for excitement. With carbon fiber frames, the bikes are light and with electric torque. WHEW, HOLD ON! With so few moving parts, electrics are almost maintenance-free. The top speed of these is about one hundred kph, plenty for city riding. You can get faster ones, though. This Chinese one is the most popular in Bangkok. It has a 150 KW motor that will stand the bike up on its back wheel with a quick twist of the throttle."

"It looks just like the one Kiet rides," Angela said. "Sweet!"

Angela purchased the bike and received the keys. In addition, Kiet received a Tee-shirt emblazoned with the bike's logo as a thank-you for his referral. The salesman then asked Angela if she would like a T-shirt.

"They are slightly clingy," he ventured. But, of course Angela wanted one. She looked streamlined in the T-shirt as she mounted her new bike and struck out on her first ride. *My God, the acceleration! Easy, girl, This isn't your old two-stroker. This bike will stand up and throw me if I hit it too hard!*

"I thought we'd head for the Sathorn Thaksin bridge and boat pier to watch the river traffic," Kiet said. "You'll see lots of Bangkok along the way. Then, we'll be back in time to chat up the Surgicenter doctors at *Tii Baan's* welcoming party."

En route, they joined other riders who steered between lines of cars and worked their way up to the stoplight. When the light turned green, about thirty bikes blew across the intersection in a wall of smoke and racket. Not yet used to her bike's power, Angela shot across the intersection on her back wheel before her front wheel settled to the pavement and whirred along with the herd.

"Yahoo! That was some wheelie!" shouted Kiet above the roar.

As they rode on, Kiet pointed to the Red Cross Institute's snake farm and vivarium. While stopped at the next light, he told Angela, "Yep, a snake farm in the middle of the city! Thailand has bout two hundred species, and about seven thousand venomous snakebites occur yearly, but only thirty deaths! Thai people refuse the old-time remedies nowadays because venom-specific antisera for most indigenous snakes are available. In fact, the Institute makes them, conducts basic research, and presents public educational programs. We'll have to see a snake show someday."

Kiet and Angela skirted a sex trade district and dodged through a jam of male tourists. "I'll tell you about Patpong, Soi Cowboy, and Nana Plaza later," he called to her. After navigating more corners and intersections, they arrived at the Saphan Thaksin bridge spanning the Chao Phraya River, Thailand's 'River of Kings'. They parked and locked their motorcycles with myriad others in a nearby lot. The pier beneath the bridge was always noisy, with a welter of tourists, kiosks dispensing tickets, river tour hawkers, and boat drivers.

The pier provided the best place to view the river's commerce and famous hotels. Tourists always hung around, looking up and down the river at lux hotels, restaurants, and high-rise condos. They watched the variety of boats going about their ordinary activities. Boats of the retro-Thai design served riverside hotels. Others were long, open-air models with colorful awnings that shielded passengers from the unsparing sun. Official mail boats churned pier to pier, carrying mail and passengers, and the sleek long-tail boats skimmed along the water.

The long-tail boats appeared adrenalized and eager for action, whether tethered to the dock or parting the waters at speed. Angela thought. They looked almost arrogant with proud glossy bodies, big engines, and long driveshafts. Polished paint jobs in blues, reds, yellows, and greens accented the lines of the boats. From the prows hung strings of flowers and religious iconography. These vessels flared rooster tails at speed, and their straight pipe exhausts roared with authority. Their prows curved haughtily skyward, appearing even tumescent to Angela. *Those boats are sexy!* They spoke to her of speed and agility while rocking with the currents and bumping rhythmically against the dock.

Definitely sexy. There's that Texas Boca Chica beach feeling again with Juan strumming and thumping his guitar in languorous rhythm, whispering his song to me, gulf waves lapping on the sand, the milky way hanging across the black sky...and everything, Angela thought. *If boats seem sexy, I guess it's been a while.*

But that one is not sexy; it looks menacing: A glossy black long-tail, an orange flame pattern streaking its sides and enveloping its aft, broke Angela's reverie. A vulture icon hung on its prow, something dead in its beak. It was docked apart from the others.

"That one is out of place," Angela said to Kiet.

"I agree. Makes me wonder who the owner is."

Drivers were hanging around their boats, hawking tours for customers, and joking back and forth. A driver with a white Thai smile bounced onto the pier from his tricolored long tail, waved, and shouted, "Hey, Kiet!"

"Hi, Wanarak, you old river rat. How's it going?" responded Kiet, exchanging wais. "You've got to meet Angela. She is not a *farang*. She's half American but was born in Ubon Ratchathani, and we went to school together. When her mother died, her dad sent her to live with an aunt in Texas in the United States. She got through med school there, but now she's back."

"Good to meet you, Wanarak," said Angela with a friendly wai. "Is that beauty your boat?"

"Good to meet you too, Angela. Any friend of this wounded old Muay is a friend of mine," said Wanarak. "Yeah, this is my boat. My father and I built it ourselves in Krabi, south of here. It's nine meters long and 2.5 meters at the widest point. It is all wood—merawan and meranti, nails, epoxy glue—looks light but weighs about two tons. The engine is a high revving monster from a wrecked Toyota."

"Wanarak and I trained together for a few months until he fell in love with life on the river," Kiet said. "I've told him about Team Bangkok, and we can count on him for help."

"Here's my number and email. We'll take a river tour together another day." Wanarak jumped into his long-tail and roared off, its rooster-tail a rainbow on that sunny day.

Angela swung astride her new bike and turned it on as they were leaving. Suddenly a guy wearing a black headband, heavy boots, and jeans hitched beneath his belly and pulled in front of her. He revved his motor and leered.

"What's a girlie *farang* in a nice T-shirt doing here on an electric bike?" he said in terrible English through a nicotine sneer.

"Get out of my way," she growled at him.

"Oh, a mixed breed, or what, speaking Thai? Come on down to the pier and ride in my boat, honey. It's black as night and flaming orange—smoking. Why don't you let me check out your electric first?" he said.

Kiet kept his distance, awaiting Angela's response.

"Like I said. Get your ass out of my way," she growled.

The guy cut his engine and hiked his leg up to dismount. Bad choice. Angela hit the throttle. The electric motor hissed, and the bike rose upon its rear wheel like a cobra preparing to strike and lunged forward. She released the throttle and hit the brakes. The front wheel struck the guy's leg, knocking him and his bike to the ground. He screeched beneath its weight.

"You gonna tell the cops that a half-breed *farang* girl took you down? I don't think so," Angela said and grinned at Kiet.

"That was kick-ass, like riding a Bangkok bronco!" said Kiet. They high-fived.

"I do like electric motorcycles," she smiled, feeling entirely electric herself. "Let's get on back to *Tii Baan*, Kiet."

8. A Gala at Tii Baan

That night at *Tii Baan* Chua hosted the Surgicenter staff for a welcoming get-together to meet the doctors and introduce Angela, the newly licensed Thai physician.

Julian DuBois arrived punctually at 7:00 p.m. and introduced himself, "I am Julian DuBois. Thank you very much for this nice welcome. It is a pleasure to meet you, Chua and Milo, and, of course, to congratulate Dr. Tran. I'm a surgeon by training and currently the chief of our small staff," he said amid universal wais. "Please, you must visit the hospital soon...not as patients, of course," he chuckled. "Allow me, *s'il vous plait*, to introduce Dr. Hu Chen." Dr. Hu had just entered the restaurant. "Dr. Hu's a vascular surgeon and heads our transplant team."

Hu was wiry and graceful. A thin mustache decorated his upper lip. Smiling tightly and surrounded by the hospital operating room staff, Hu reminded Milo of a Khmer general entering *Tii Baan* with his retinue. Hu introduced his chief operating room nurse, Mina, and her staff. As Hu bent slightly forward to wai, his scrub shirt fell away, and Angela saw a tattoo just under his collarbone that looked like a zombie, the same figure decorating his scrub shirt pocket. *That's a weird logo for a surgeon. I wonder what his story is.*

Chua and Milo introduced themselves and welcomed their guests. "Dr. Tran is an American doctor born in Thailand and new to the Bangkok medical community. She is staying at the PIP tower," said Milo.

"She was a child when her father and I worked together in Ubon Ratchathani. After her mother died, Angela moved to Texas and eventually worked her way through college and medical school doing Thai translations. Then she shed her skin again and returned to Thailand.

"She just received her Thai medical license today, so tonight is a celebration."

"Very impressive, Khun Doctor Angela," Julian said and executed a playfully elaborate wai.

"The pleasure is mine, and please call me Angela," she smiled. "Do I hear a trace of a foreign accent?"

"You have a refined ear, Angela," Julian said. "I was born in Vietnam, but my family moved to Thailand immediately after Dien Bien Phu and settled in Nong Khai across the Mekong from Vientiane, where French is a common language."

"How interesting. So, it's French that accents your elegant Thai."

"Yes. Thai people can still hear my accent. My parents sent me to live with an aunt in Aix-en-Provence in the south of France because of tough times when I was a child. When I got back, my parents sat me down at the dinner table with a stern teacher, who drummed Thai into me for hours on end. It's my daily language now. Why don't we have a glass of wine before dinner and talk about non-medical things?"

"Let's do," Angela said as they moved toward the bar. "I was born near Ubon Ratchathani and grew up on an Air Force base during the Pol Pot years. My parents were intelligence officers in that nest of spies, as some Khmer Rouge called it. Mom was a doctor too, a flight surgeon. She worked in nearby villages during her free time throughout her pregnancy. One afternoon her water broke, and a midwife delivered me in a village clinic, making me a Thai citizen. And now about that wine?"

"Ah, yes, the wine."

Milo had turned on the stereo and queued up "Hotel California." He selected a lovely rosé, wrapped a napkin around the bottle sommelier style, poured a sample, and asked Julian if it was to his taste.

"It most certainly is, *merci*, Milo," said Julian, after a swirl and sniff. "Ah, 'Hotel California,'" he said, smiling at Angela. "It seems Milo may have had a taste of wine already."

Julian sipped his wine and sang along softly with the stereo, mixing memorized English with French-flavored Thai, 'I wanted to stay in that hotel. They said I could check out but could never leave.' I can feel the poetry even if I don't understand English, Angela. You must feel it even more deeply."

Angela swirled her glass to keep from dropping it. *My God, the man's flirting. I do feel the poetry.* Then, with a catch in her breath, she responded, "I've never heard 'Hotel California' with a French accent."

"Confidentially, a French accent is handy sometimes," Julian smiled and wiggled his brows.

"Well, now."

They continued their dinner by candlelight, a definite first for *Tii Baan*, like Milo's sommelier parody and the checkered tablecloths on wooden tabletops.

Lingering over a glass of sweet dessert wine, Julian smiled and asked her thoughts as a Texan about cobras compared to rattlesnakes.

"Texans always asked me the opposite question," Angela said. "So, both rattlers and cobras have forked tongues and bite, much like humans."

Julian wondered aloud which type he might be. And which she might be.

To that, Angela just smiled.

As Julian and Dr. Hu Chen said their goodbyes, Angela said, "I'd like to see the Surgicenter and talk about possible openings on the staff."

"Tomorrow's not a surgery day," Julian said. "So let me show you around. We can meet here and walk over."

When Julian and Dr. Hu Chen headed out of the restaurant toward the Surgicenter, Julian paused and said, "A cobra, maybe?"

The night was young, and the team's spirits were still high. So, they cleaned up the restaurant, brought the closed-for-special-event sign in from the sidewalk, and lowered the shutter. They talked about the party.

"We were all watching you and Julian," Milo said. "Looks like you two hit it off. Of course, we've got it on video in case—."

"You are such snoops!" said Angela smiling. "We had fun. Julian flirted with his charming French accent and made me laugh. He's the sort of company that a girl enjoys."

"Oh là là," said Milo, "the French charm, eh Angela?"

"Oh, stop it, Milo! What about you, playing sommelier? And were the candles and checkered tablecloths your preposterous idea?" asked Angela.

"That aside," she continued, "Julian's back story is interesting. His family is natively French but lived in Vietnam until the Geneva Settlement when Julian was a toddler. They settled in Thailand across from Vientiane, Laos, because of their French language and culture. Being *farangs*, his parents struggled to get a start. Later they sent Julian to live with an aunt in France. Thus, his French accent.

"Anyhow, when Julian returned to Thailand, he did well in school. He graduated from Chulalongkorn University in medicine with high honors. He wiggled his eyebrows, wondering if he was more like a cobra or rattler. I need to decide because he invited me to tour the Surgicenter tomorrow."

"As snoops go, I have an admission to make," said Milo. "Wisut and Kiet dropped by the Surgicenter for a bit of surveillance while dinner was going on."

"Yes," Kiet said. "The Surgicenter was dark except for bluish light behind the doctors' office windows coming from computer monitors. We continued scouting from the back alley, where the light of a single bulb faded across the loading dock. But again, there was nothing suspicious, no ambulance or guard shack."

"Nothing suspicious at all," Wisut agreed, "so my guys later checked the Surgicenter's computers—all ordinary except for some Virtual Reality surgery stuff on Dr. Hu's. Otherwise, it was pretty boring.

"However, earlier today, my guys installed facial recognition software on our server and also made the city's administrative records transparent—building permits for the facility, financing, ownership—that sort of thing. I don't teach hacking in the department but encourage it for noble purposes and the postdocs' enjoyment."

"Noble, are we now?" said Angela. "Or amateurs playing sleuth, creeping around in the dark, setting sensors, hacking computers?"

"You're right," Milo said. "Software can't do it all. That's where you come in. When you tour the Surgicenter tomorrow, you'll be our 'feet on the ground'.

9. The Surgicenter Revealed

Julian and Angela met for coffee at *Tii Baan* before touring the Surgicenter.

"Congratulations on that Thai license!" Julian said. "You just walked in and got it in one day. That's unheard of; So, really, congratulations!"

"Thanks, but I had already passed the examinations online, so there was no red tape. Khun Noi—she's chief of Bangkok's medical board—and I had a nice conversation. It turns out that she studied for several years in Texas. She enjoys speaking English and is quite fluent. It's fabulous to see a woman in this important position in Thailand."

"I'll bet you talked about more than medicine—probably a pleasure for you both."

"Yes, thank goodness," Angela said as they headed to the Surgicenter next door. "We reminisced about Texas, chit-chatted about the medical community in Bangkok, and compared the hot weather in Texas and Thailand. Dr. Noi is a clever lady who keeps her finger on the pulse of the medical community."

"That's important during today's social and technological changes in medicine," Julian said.

Julian gestured theatrically as they arrived at the Surgicenter entrance. "Welcome to the Surgicenter, Angela." They passed an empty waiting area and a vacant administrative desk. As their steps echoed through the hall, Angela asked, "Where is all the usual hospital hubbub? Empty halls, no overhead pages, no nurses or orderlies hurrying by, and no action? How do you keep the doors open?"

"Don't you hear the hammers and drills? We are expanding at breakneck speed. The specialty center concept has caught on, and new doctors are beating the doors down for staff privileges. Specialists like a dialysis group, cosmetic surgeons, ophthalmologists, and orthopaedists have applied. Their practice requirements are varied, and we plan to accommodate them all. So, we aren't seeing patients for the time being. But, you'll see a renovated Surgicenter soon. I hope you'll consider practicing here with us."

"But I'm not a specialist."

"That's your great advantage, Angela. Specialists always have a tight focus and appreciate having a big-picture generalist standing by to help. That would be you."

"For example, Hu and I have scheduled several transplants the day the doors open. We'd want you to help manage their medical conditions. Most of them have diabetes and require medical management. In case you are wondering, this is a formal invitation for you to join us. Should I fit you for a white coat?"

"I am thrilled, Julian, of course. It's an exciting offer. I'll need to think about it. But let's do check out coat sizes." They paused to look at patient rooms and strolled toward the women's changing area. While trying on several white coats, Angela recoiled. "What's that horrible figure on that coat's pocket all about?"

"That's Hu's scrub nurse's coat, and the horrible figure is *Jaingshi*. He's the mythological hopping zombie, the reanimated corpse of a person who died from foul play. He has risen in a state of rigor mortis with muscles so stiff that he can only hop. In Chinese horror stories and movies, Jaingshi seeks hideous revenge for his murder."

"Yuk, I saw Hu's tattoo. I want to avoid Jaingshi. Should I keep looking over my shoulder?"

"No worries. However, Jaingshi has been Dr. Hu's terror for years. Jaingshi's tattooed on his chest and stenciled on his scrub shirt pocket, and I can only surmise why.

"Hu was raised upcountry in a world of animism and spiritual phenomena and still holds some arcane beliefs, even as a doctor. He's also hardcore into martial arts, as if kung fu could fight off zombies!" Julian chuckled.

"Given his build, I can believe he's into martial arts. Is he made of springs?"

"Yeah, he's quick, wiry, and really stern on the outside," said Julian. "But inside? Well, one night, Hu drove us to see his parents upcountry. He slammed on the brakes when a tree rose through the fog, its limbs draping over a rice paddy like extended arms. He froze momentarily and murmured something about woodland spirits."

"You are giving me chills."

"I occasionally get chills, too, but Hu's an outstanding surgeon. Rest assured, Jaingshi's not a hospital logo, and he won't be on your white coat."

"Thank goodness."

"So, back to our earlier conversation, Angela. Our founders are patient and committed to excellence. They are willing to slow the Surgicenter operations down and temporarily close the doors for renovations as long as we recruit top doctors. Our doctors' practices must meet the American Joint Commission on Accreditation standards because most of our transplant patients come from Western countries and usually expect an independent review of standards.

"The owners understand Hu is a top doctor, a natural surgeon, quick mind, skilled hands, and commitment to learning new techniques. I think the owners will support us as long as Hu is in action. Hu plans to go places."

"What about you?"

Julian swallowed and said, "I'm an excellent laparoscopic surgeon. I do gallbladders, appendices, hernias, and other intra-abdominal and minor thoracic procedures. Also, I'm a bariatric surgeon, but how many fat Thai people do you see? I aim to build a reputation in laparoscopy in Bangkok, but the competition is fierce."

As they toured the operating rooms, Julian said, "I always team with Hu on kidney transplant procedures. I retrieve a donor's kidney laparoscopically in my OR and pass it straight to Hu in the adjacent OR for implantation in the recipient."

"It sounds like a textbook set-up for efficiency and safety," Angela said, thinking, *Everything is top-of-the-line. There is no space here for a cardiac unit.*

Julian pointed out the recovery room, CAT scanner, and MRI as they continued down the hall. As Julian and Angela neared the laboratory, workers were installing dialysis machines in a new section.

"The new center will complete our full-service kidney efforts with a dialysis unit run by local nephrologists," explained Julian. "We provide transplantation services for both Thai people and patients from abroad. In Thailand, family members generally donate kidneys for their relatives."

"So, where do the kidneys for foreigners come from?"

"There are no altruistic kidney donors for foreigners. Instead, our sponsors purchase kidneys locally from poor people for our international transplant patients," said Julian.

"Aren't you concerned that current international transplantation conventions condemn kidney commerce? Thailand is signing on. How do you handle that?"

"It's complex, Angela, as you know. Many cultural, ethical, moral, and religious issues are in play, so it's a complicated landscape to navigate. First, the international codes themselves have led to long lists of patients throughout the West awaiting transplants. Most are on dialysis and stay hooked to a machine forever or die before their number comes up. At the same time, many needy people will readily sell a kidney. It's mutually beneficial. Transplants shorten the waiting lists for Western patients, and our poor will be wealthier. We see this as ethically responsible and economically viable—a win-win.

"Also, our local donors don't relate to the formal medical declarations. Most of them consider 'WEIRD" to mean 'Western, Educated, Industrialized, Rich, Democratic' countries, if I understand the words, with few abjectly poor people. That's my take on it, too, as a doctor working on the ground with real patients—donors and recipients—nothing abstract about that."

"Oh, yes, that 'WEIRD'. I've never heard it applied to organ sales, but I get the point. Fair enough, particularly as a cultural go-by."

"Also, helping the poor and unfortunate is a tenant of Buddhism. Buddhists believe that donating an organ that gives life to another deserves great merit. Our sponsors are down-to-earth realists and definitely in step with the local community's cultural and religious values.

"For example, as they planned the Surgicenter, the founders had a Brahmin priest officiate at the Surgicenter's foundation ceremony to situate the building site properly before construction began.

"They also sought the advice of the local Temple and the Monastery about cultural issues and developed essential guidelines together. First, potential donors would confer with a monk and request their advice before registering with us. These discussions would rule out possible exploitation and ensure that the donor's choice is informed and voluntary. Donors can confer with a monk or withdraw at any time, including at the last minute if asked to donate.

"We get second opinions from outside doctors to ensure donors are medically fit. Then we ensure potential donors have two functioning kidneys, for goodness sake. And we repeat a medical examination ourselves immediately before surgery. This measure would fall into your bailiwick. We also keep an accurate, up-to-date database of each donor's health, blood and tissue types, and demographic profiles.

"Am I going on too long?"

"Not at all. I appreciate your thoroughness."

"Our owners notify the government authorities of our general activities annually and have never encountered push-back. Municipal hospital safety inspections are conducted quarterly. Everything is on the up and up. The owners also contribute a small amount to the Temple for every kidney purchased. Transplant tourism is common here. We think our operation is the cleanest and best in Bangkok."

Angela digested this for a moment—she appreciated their guidelines. Still, she decided to discuss the ethical considerations with Milo and Noi. As they continued through the hospital, Angela observed a lab with an automated blood analysis system. She realized that the Surgicenter was a first-class facility and felt herself buying into the entire concept.

As they passed along the doctors' offices, Angela noted two computers in Hu's office. Hu wore a mesh cap. "Hu, say hello to Angela," said Julian.

Hu waied, took off his virtual reality headset, and said, "I hope you're enjoying your visit, Angela. Pretty neat place, huh? We need a generalist and hope you will join us. Have you watched much VR surgery?"

"I saw some amazing VR cases during my internship and thought VR will become more important as medical teaching devices, especially for surgery."

Hu said, "Yes, our programs in Thailand have VR set-ups. The sights and sounds are so realistic in surgery that it's like watching a live procedure. Julian and I video our procedures. I think it has made us better surgeons."

"Watching your own surgery must help improve your technique."

"It does. I also have a library of VR surgical procedures, including some fabulous ones of children's heart surgery from your Massachusetts General Hospital," said Hu. "I watch them all the time. You can use my library whenever you wish."

She thanked Hu for the offer, and as they were leaving Hu's office, Julian said, "I enjoy VR but don't geek out on it like Hu does."

Overhearing this, Hu laughed. "I 'geek out', do I? What an expression. But it's so true."

As they continued down the hall, Julian said, "Hu is intrigued by the idea of seamlessly merging reality and virtual reality. To develop a participatory VR system, he works with a Chinese software company, SinoAI. It's in the planning stages now, but when developed, a surgeon can perform VR surgery from skin to skin! So it won't be just watching; it'll be doing. Also, they hope to have an expert avatar to offer suggestions or technical assistance. SinoAI is clearly on the, uh, 'bleeding' edge of surgical virtual reality."

"That sounds like a big step up from just watching a virtual reality video."

"The Congress of Asian Surgeons thinks so too. In fact, they have invited Hu to present his work in Beijing this spring as the keynote speaker. He's up at all hours of the night working the bugs out and traveling to China on weekends."

By late afternoon, Angela had toured the facility. She now understood why Julian and Hu choose to work here. The futuristic feeling of the place attracted her. Drs. Julian and Hu consider it the best environment to develop as surgeons: Julian as Bangkok's top laparoscopic surgeon, Hu to follow his talents and ambitions if Jaingshi got out of the way. And excellent opportunities for her ongoing professional development.

As she left, Angela asked Julian to join her at *Tii Baan* for a glass of wine. He begged off with a friendly wai and said goodbye, adding, "Hu and I have a lunch meeting with our owners at *Tii Baan* tomorrow. Maybe a glass of wine together afterward?"

An important day for Angela was ending. Her spirits were high. Great colleagues and a great first job offer for this new Thai doctor.

She phoned Milo. His phone was busy, so she left a message, "Heart surgery at Siam Surgicenter is not possible," she said. "I'm taking the job, but not as a spy."

A fleeting rain had washed the dust from the trees along Soi Rangnam. As the sun sank, the air was clear as polished glass, the sidewalks were dry, and the street shimmered black with wisps of surface mist. Customers at *Tii Baan* were settling in for the evening's conviviality. The ceiling fans stirred delicious aromas, and the beer was cold. English, Thai, Chinese, and other languages harmonized in the general murmur. Spirits were high as the customers enjoyed an early evening's launch to wherever.

Angela sat at the 'VIP' table where she could people-watch and ordered a cold Singha.

10. Not a Spy

Angela was still people-watching when Milo, Kiet, and Wisut drifted in and sat down with her. Angela recapped the events of her big day and stressed her refusal to spy.

"Are you hearing this, guys?" Milo said. "Angela is legal. She got her license today and an offer from the Surgicenter. So congratulations! And she's certain that heart surgery is impossible at the facility: kidney transplants, corneas, etc., yes, but hearts, no."

"Thanks," said Angela. "The Surgicenter is impressive. Its founders touched all the medical and cultural bases before starting the business. They ensured complete medical care for donors, support from the local religious leaders, and a bit of income for the monks. I also learned they provide some anonymous support for Dow's clinic. Hu and Julian are forward-looking surgeons and true believers in specialty practices. We don't have to investigate the Siam Surgicenter. It's on the up-and-up."

Milo added, "And Angela is not a spy."

"Right, Milo, I'm already feeling a little guilty about visiting on false pretenses; still, I am happy for the opportunity. I really like Julian. He is what I call a real doc. For him, patients are people, and he respects their concerns. I like his sense of humor: it's subtle. For example, he punned that Hu gets a serious kick out of martial arts. He also joked that Kung Fu couldn't defeat Hu's zombies. Also, that Hu 'geeks out'. I love that expression. In truth, Hu is developing a Virtual Reality system for surgeons."

"Virtual is big. Most of my colleagues believe AI will usher in the next epoch for mankind," Wisut said. "Including surgery too, I'd guess."

"Yes, well. Julian thinks Hu is brilliant," Angela continued. "It's hard to understand why Hu wears this weird Jaingshi logo, but he's quite remarkable apart from that little quirk. Actually, Hu reminds me of Dr. Stern; intelligent and very engaging. I sense those traits in Julian too, but he is too modest to brag.

"They make an effective team," Angela said. "Perhaps Team Bangkok should consider recruiting them when the right time is right."

"Men of character and skill, are they?" Milo said. "We'll have to keep an eye on them. Their surgical knowledge and language skills could be important to us. I'll mention this to our UN manager.

"By the way, the Surgicenter's owners are dropping by for lunch tomorrow with the docs. We'll join them remotely with our digital assets. Wisut, can your White Hats check out the bosses afterward?"

"Yes, and if anyone is worried about our surveillance methods, the UN says we're legit with the Thai government."

"Good point," said Milo and closed the evening with, "Remember, what's not virtual is the likelihood that another heart is on its way to Bangkok."

11. Milo's Rant

Before leaving for *Tii Baan* the next morning, Angela saw the *Bangkok Scimitar's* overnight opinion piece.

Last week, we displayed an extraordinary photograph: A heart in the street on a bed of ice that fell from a delivery box during a motorbike wreck. The photo has gone viral. It's blanketing the world in every medium, as is this narrative: Today, somewhere in an Asian country lies a corpse of a young person emptied of its heart, an innocent person, probably plucked from an ethnic minority and murdered, whose family now grieves, as does the world in sympathy. We believe that person's heart was destined for transplantation commerce and have learned that an elderly Western woman, possibly enfeebled by heart failure, has not met her scheduled flight home. Was the heart intended for her? Speculation is growing.

The Editors

Angela had a quick coffee and juice and then headed to *Tii Baan*. Milo was having his morning coffee and holding forth to everyone within hearing range his commentary on the *Scimitar's* article.

She said, "Good morning, Milo."

Milo's rant over the *Scimitar's* report continued. "It's about time the paper catches on. Everybody else has. The public already knows that someone stole a heart, kept it alive somehow, and shipped it to a covert operating room in Bangkok. Last-mile motorcycle delivery was stupid, and the smugglers will figure another way next time. So public emotions are amping up everywhere."

"Well, like I said, 'Hello, Milo'!"

Milo muttered to himself, "We have lots of footwork to do – inspection of landing permits at Don Muang Airport, for one thing."

Then, he looked up from the paper. "Oh, hello Angela, good that you're here."

Wisut's quick steps sounded as he rushed in. "Good morning, Milo, Angela. I see you're reading the *Scimitar*. I think their assumptions are rational and correct. I just got off the Skytrain. From what people were saying, I believe a mighty shit storm is gathering over Bangkok."

"No doubt the public has already caught on, and its mood is sour. I hope the *Scimitar* will resist stirring up emotions any further," said Milo, and Angela nodded in agreement. "What luck did you have yesterday, Wisut?"

"I phoned the *Scimitar's* reporter, and was she ever swamped! She confirmed, however, that an elderly lady has overstayed her visa—true, whether or not related to our speculations. But unfortunately, she didn't share anything more. So, I contacted Customs and Immigration and learned that the lady in question left the airport with the RFC's luxury package group. Altogether, no luck. So I unleashed the White Hats to investigate digitally.

"They located the Grande Dame's picture and personal details. She left the airport with a Royal Facets Complex Luxury Package group. That much is certain. There is more.

A postdoc thought to check the vehicle traffic heading in the Surgicenter's direction and interrogated the corner traffic camera. She saw a blue TopazEV pass by several times but didn't get a good photo of the driver. So she combed our Thailand automobile files for the driver's photo. Unfortunately, it's not there, indicating he's probably not a Thai citizen."

"Yeah," echoed Kiet, who had just wandered in. "I've seen the TopazEV, too. It caught my attention. It's an expensive car to just be driving around and might be the only one in Bangkok. So that triggered my sixth sense."

"Okay, Kiet, I'm not sure where it takes us, but we'll keep that in mind," said Milo.

Wisut said, "The engineers and pediatricians at Chulalongkorn confirm the device found at the scene is a mini-pump oxygenator."

"Great work, Wisut. That implies sophisticated engineering, which Burma doesn't have," said Milo, "and keeps China in the conversation.

"I've only seen TopazEVs on the Internet, Kiet. So, keep your eyes open."

12. Creatures from Former Times

In a little-known bar tucked away beneath a prominent hotel on Bangkok's famous Sukhumvit Road, sports play interminably on large screens, beers run cold on draft, and short orders are spectacular. Its singular clientele expects absolute discretion and gets it. Their exchanges fade like ghosts into the smoky air.

Two old friends relaxed behind a pitcher of Singha beer in a back corner, holding an owners' meeting for their singularly brilliant medical creation, the Siam Surgicenter, a specialty surgical hospital.

Boc and Khem had been semi-gangsters in their younger years but grew into refined *Chao pho*, Mafia-like bureaucrats working in downtown Bangkok. Refined, if not wholly reformed. They recalled their long-gone days as 'testosterone times' of vigor, danger, and excitement.

Boc, a Thai national, had worked with the government and international philanthropies as a young man. Representing the Thai Ministry of Defense, he had helped build Khao I Dang, the first border camp for Cambodian refugees fleeing the genocide in Pol Pot's "New Cambodia". After Khao I Dang opened, refugees poured over 100,000 a year into Thailand. More camps sprang up in Thailand under Boc's direction; with them, more money to build and sustain them poured through his hands. Some stuck. Who would know?

Starving bellies, torn and diseased bodies, and broken souls crossed the border from the killing fields into the camps, and shady characters and black marketers thrived in the chaos.

Good and bad guys and others in between, Western and Asian, exploited the chaos: Good-guy types, the NGOs, missionaries, medical volunteers, and experts offering counsel and assistance. Or bad guys, spies, and others trading in narcotics, gems, children, and arms. Furtive whispers traded state secrets in wooden shacks and other places shadowed from the light of day. Thai officials sold visas to those who could afford them. Someone even offered a stinger missile for sale. They all mingled in the shabby chaos.

During those years, Khem, a young Cambodian national, engaged in log smuggling operations that required extensive knowledge of the region's geography. If you wanted to buy teak, you saw Khem. His routes led him around the Dangrek mountains near Anlong Veng, a village close to the Thai border and dangerously near Pol Pot's encampment. Fortunately, Pot offered Khem safe passage in exchange for tending to Pot's personal needs from Thailand—food, mainly maize and rice, clothing and boots, medications, plus a cut of Khem's profits. Khem considered these cuts small prices to pay for his business's survival. Even after Pot dipped in, the logging profits were enormous. Moreover, his profits increased as Thai government officials playing both sides of the war used Khem's connection with the dictator.

Boc built several sawmills to cut the lumber needed for construction in the camps and purchased the logs from Khem. They got to know each other and discovered mutual interests. Boc persuaded Khem to part with 49% of his logging business in exchange for a permanent Thai visa, convertible quickly to citizenship. Their partnership prospered, nourished in the chaotic border broth. Later, they expanded into dealing visas and other non-lethal lines of work. But the logging business remained the most lucrative of all.

As time passed, consorting with danger became less adrenalized and eventually downright scary. Boc and Khem had plenty of money and profitable connections that led to Thai government employment. Their administrative hands touched customs and immigration, transportation, building and land management, and other intangibles more valuable than commodities. They kept their logging business but avoided trade in humans, drugs, and prostitution—things that can get you killed, thank you. Instead, white-collar activities—administrative legerdemain, blackmail, influence peddling, contracting, and business managed by phone—kept them busy and safe. Now, after many years, they could kick back and ruminate on the good old days.

Enjoying his first pint of Singha, Khem said, "Doing business back then was easy. Load up some elephants, bring the logs down to trucks, grease some palms, skirt the fighting, and sell the logs. Pay off Pot's men and head back for some more logs. But always mind your own business.

"I don't feel sorry for him, but Pol Pot didn't have it easy," Khem continued, "cooped up in Anlong Veng, sicker than shit, afraid Vietnamese and government forces might show up any time and kill his ass. I watched him strut around his pitiful stronghold in his black pajama outfit and red-checked scarf, lecturing his bored lieutenants, who had heard it all before. I saw Ta Mok there, too, before he put Pot under house arrest. Ta Mok frequently crossed the border and spoke with Americans."

"I heard that the US quietly supported the Khmer Rouge for a period while the Vietnamese were invading Cambodia," said Boc. "Some higher-ups said that Ta Mok sent feelers to the US, offering to turn Pol Pot over to them for something, who knows what? So there's loyalty for you."

"I believe it," Khem said, "I saw Ta Mok meet with several US intelligence types and a slick-looking muckety-muck American at Chao Dang 1. He spoke perfect Cambodian. The US didn't buy into Ta Mok's offer. Maybe we'll know what happened in twenty or thirty years when the documents come out.

"I remember both of those bastards, Pot and Ta Mok," Khem went on. "Pot died from 'heart failure' in 1998—that's the official line anyhow—and never made it to the Khmer Rouge Tribunals. But I believe he either committed suicide or was poisoned. Rumors had it that Ta Mok got 'medicine' from a lady doctor, maybe some poison.

"Ta Mok's still in jail waiting his turn on the Tribunal docket. He's always jabbering to the press about how he helped poor Cambodians and proclaiming his innocence. They say the murderous son-of-a-bitch may die before he gets what he deserves. I've wondered if the land mine that blew his leg off might have taken his balls off too."

"Maybe that's what makes him so mean," mused Boc.

Having aged up, Boc and Khem were respected as old-timers among Asia's Mafia syndicates. They belonged to the Council of Elders, composed of grizzled former leaders of transnational Asian crime syndicates. This Council reduced conflicts among the loosely associated racketeers and influenced the growth and sophistication of their operations.

Boc and Khem craved one final, lucrative venture as compulsory government retirement approached. They had set up The Siam Surgicenter a few years back for the thrill of it. That had been an excellent project, and they had done it right.

"The Siam Surgicenter seems like a religious experience to me. Helping the poor while bringing kidneys to the desperate rich, who'd otherwise spend the rest of their days hooked up to dialysis machines," Khem said, sipping his latest pint of Singha. "The sick and desperate supporting the poor and needy, with our help. We're doing well while doing good. It's downright transmogrifying."

"Where   in   the   hell   did   you   get   that   word —Trans-damn-morgrifying?"

"I'm still expanding my Thai vocabulary, Boc. Just thought I'd try it out on you after a couple of beers to get your reaction," chuckled Khem. "And I did."

As the evening wore on, they fell back into their earlier mood and exchanged sentimental toasts to past times. "Looking back, it was easier then—ticklish with old Pol Pot— but easier. We were young. Life was good," concluded Boc as they asked for the bill. "What's next? Who knows?" They continued to chat.

Boc picked up the line, "Avoiding the drug trade, that was smart. The heroin king from Burma/Thailand, Khun Sa, was a dangerous man to cross, even accidentally. Afghanistan came along and took a bite from the heroin market. Then yaba and Fentanyl appeared, cheap to make, easy to smuggle. And a magnet for the new Mafia trash. They've seen too many movies. So, they've brought violence and mayhem with them. They don't respect their elders. They are dangerous, leg breakers, killers. New drugs, very profitable but not safe."

"Yeah, we were lucky. We came up in good times: Things just opened up for us after Cambodia. Making money with money. Laundering got better as the world got richer. Wash your money in real estate deals, Cambodian seaside deals, and casinos: there's the big money today. Our people have gotten smoother, grooming themselves in respectability, image building, and affecting legitimate faces. And richer too for all of that. Our Mafia children get university educations nowadays, become lawyers, businessmen, and the like. It's a cleaner picture internationally. Our top syndicates support each other. Altogether it's nearly bloodless," Khem said.

Boc said, "We are maintaining a kind of homeostasis. As a man of fine words, Khem, you probably know homeostasis means internal balance and stable equilibrium. I learned it from our kidney surgeons. Smooth operations, good relations with officialdom, satisfied donors and recipients. Harmony. But this 'heart on ice' thing could blow the equilibrium apart. I worry."

"You mean it will destabilize the homeostasis, you pretentious butt hole," joked Khem. "There's danger out there; I feel it too. Somebody's bringing serious evil. I'm afraid they are already here, given the *Scimitar* photo. There's going to be a public opinion shitstorm. It will smudge us all. "Mafia, Mafia, Mafia, everyone will think 'birds of a feather'. They will tar the good guys like us with the same brush. There go our friends. All because of a motorcycle wreck, a heart, and a missing old lady."

"She's missing, all right," Khem agreed.

"She will stay missing unless they bring in another heart."

"It's not our problem, except it probably is."

"Maybe, the Siam Surgicenter is our last big thing," said Boc. "Maybe there won't be a next big thing."

"Maybe, maybe not, but our world will change. This heart business could blow a hole in our businesses, scare off our local benefactors and ruin our international enterprises. Our next big thing may be restoring our vaunted 'homeostasis'".

"You may be right," said Boc.

They had one more for the road and stubbed out their cigarettes, ending this evening of sentimental rumination and brewing a sense of dread. They emerged onto Sukhumwit Soi, and, holding the railing, they ascended the steps to a Skytrain station and stood behind the yellow line until a train thundered into the station. They entered a frigid air-conditioned car destined for their separate condos on Sukhumvit Road. They planned to have a casual lunch with the Siam Surgicenter doctors at *Tii Baan* tomorrow.

At the Asok stop, a nondescript man brushed Boc and passed him a note.

"From my boss," he murmured and exited the car.

Boc read the note and passed it to Khem, who wrinkled his forehead. It was unsigned, but they understood. "The Council of Elders will be meeting and contacting you soon. Don't bring your phones," the note said.

13. Never Alone

Milo scooped up the last of his papaya salad just as two well-groomed gentlemen entered the restaurant. *They look like government bureaucrats nearing retirement age,* Milo thought. The doctors followed close on their heels.

"*Sawatdii khrap.* Gentlemen, Doctors. How may I help you?"

"*Sawatdii khrap,* we'd like to sit back from the street, maybe toward the back. Less noise there," Boc replied. Milo seated them, nodded the waiter off, and took their order himself.

They placed their lunch orders, Khem smacking his lips in anticipation of cold Thai tea. They fell into conversation, discussing first the new dialysis set-up. Milo stepped behind the bar to activate the cameras and microphones, placing the four under the digital scrutiny of Wisut's lab. Alerted, the White-hat team would investigate the Surgicenter's owners.

"Hu, I hope you get back to surgery soon," Khem said. "Do you need anything for the OR? We're sitting on a backlog of internationals."

"We're still finishing the renovations and checking the credentials of new specialists applying for privileges. We'll pick up the surgical pace soon and whittle that backlog down. By the way, we've met a new doctor. She is a generalist who'll make all the specialists more effective. We'd like to hire her."

"A lady doctor, huh? Well, hire her if she'll help you push things along," said Boc. "I'd like to hear more, but Khem and I have to meet a friend, so we'd better get going. Let's talk again soon."

After their fine lunch at *Tii Baan,* Boc and Khem strolled along the walkways in Lumpini Park as directed by Kimsan's note. A familiar figure approached, waied when he reached them, and the three walked on.

"Kimsan, good to see you," said Khem. "We were surprised to get your note." Kimsan was the chairman of the Council of Elders.

"Sorry I had to contact you that way, but you know how it is," Kimsan began. "Someone always listens in, tracking you everywhere. Can't trust the electronics. Cameras and eyes are everywhere. Thus, the brush-by on the Skytrain.

"It's risky for the full Council to meet in one place, so I've spoken with our other members. They agree we can consider our meeting formal. So, let's walk and talk and get lost in the crowd." Boc and Khem concurred.

Kimsan's DNA sprang from the bloodline of Cambodia's long-serving Prime Minister Hun Sen, who had run the country for twenty-five years. Blood was thick in the Sen family. Kimsan's children were educated and positioned in the heights of government, law, and finance. Kimsan was known among the financial cognoscenti for his generosity, discretion, and power.

He was president and chairman of the Commerce Bank of Cambodia (CBC) in Phnom Penh, which had gobbled up land in the city and resort areas for almost three decades. After international authorities cracked down on money laundering in Macau, Kimsan's bank took the reins of international money laundering through investments in casino complexes and real estate ventures along the frenzied Sihanoukville coast. Beneath the bank's polished veneer of financial gobbledygook lay the hard surface of transnational crime. The CBC now slithered sticky tentacles into piggy banks across the world. Much of Kimsan's personal largesse favored business relationships with China's super-rich, whose influence grew ever larger in Cambodia.

"I'm here because our *Pho Chao* syndicates are suffering from the glare of negative publicity," Kimsan said. "The media is spreading the Bangkok bruhaha across Asia, harping on 'Someone Had to Die' and

'Are There Others'?" Their constant drumming stirs suspicions that we have a hand in it. As a result, our relationships with friends in high places are wilting and crimping everyone's bottom line. So the membership is punting their concerns to the Council, insisting that we shut the media up," said Kimsan.

"The *Siam Scimitar* broke the heart-on-ice story, but nothing exciting has happened since then. So, now they only moralize and speculate. They sermonize, 'where are our authorities when we need them?'. This stirs the pot that feeds the public's negative mood," said Khem.

Boc interjected, "Even the international news organizations have launched journalists into Bangkok, looking for more ghastly news. 'Investigative reporters' are behind every tree. Lift a manhole cover, and out pops some gonzo muckraker.

"The public's in a meltdown. In ordinary times, people tolerated low-level stuff—smuggling a few logs, washing some money, moving some jewels," Boc continued. "They even enjoyed spending a few virtuous baht for the police to catch some low-level guys. That satisfied them.

"But these are not normal times. The public compares the heart debacle to big-time stuff like child pornography, bondage, drugs, etc., and they can't abide it. Somebody getting killed for their heart freaks everybody out—appropriately so. But we are not into that stuff. We don't even break legs anymore."

"Yes, Boc, we're repeating the same thing. I've whispered into important media ears," Kimsan said, "but no response is forthcoming. The editors can't be reasoned with.

"Therefore, we must solve the problem ourselves. For once, our colleagues are speaking in a single voice. For once, we are not herding cats," he continued. "Our colleagues believe an aberrant syndicate is at work and have instructed us to find it and take it out. That will require power and smarts.

"Boc, Khem, you two are the Council's Bangkok arm. You are the tip of the spear. You must find this hellish group and take them out. We stand united behind you and will provide whatever assistance you need. I know this is a daunting assignment, but we are confident in your ability to accomplish it."

"We appreciate your confidence, but—" began Khem just as Kimsan continued.

"Our confidence is well-founded. You are smart guys and have operated closer to legitimacy than any of us. You are the fathers of medical tourism in Thailand, brilliant! You can manage this assignment. Count on me for help with any requirements beyond your capabilities."

Khem responded in formal Khmer, swallowing hard, "Great words and high praise, Kimsan, and you can count on us to resolve the problem."

"I'm sure we can," said Kimsan. "Our syndicates agree with your view that Burma and China are somehow involved in different capacities. Therefore, we will provide capabilities beyond your geographic restrictions. That includes muscular leverage, of course. Just call," said Kimsan.

These good words stiffened Boc's and Khem's spines, but Kimsan had saved the best until last.

"And here is a pearl: you are not alone in Bangkok. A clandestine United Nations group known as Team Bangkok is already operating here. Like yours, their mission is to investigate the threat of international heart transplant tourism. They have planted a young woman doctor in your Surgicenter to look into possible heart work."

Khem looked incredulous, "How can you know this?"

"Our government connections extend even into the UN. We hear things. My young niece is an attaché to the UN. She says trading secrets and gossiping are the most exciting things that happen there. And Team Bangkok has been the hottest topic lately," replied Kimsan. "So you are not alone in this quest. Find this Team Bangkok. Combine forces, and get results."

"But —" said Boc.

"Yeah, strange bedfellows, this Team Bangkok, right? But remember the enemy of our enemy, etc. So join them and, together, take the bastards down fast. Be your brilliant selves, be tough."

Although left unsaid, Boc and Khem understood, "Or else". Kimsan's instruction was not a request.

They said goodbye to Kimsan, and the parties departed Lumpini Park in opposite directions.

"Yeah, right, brilliant and tough," Boc mused.

14. New Members

Later in the week, Milo invited Hu, Julian, and Angela to meet him at *Tii Baan*.

"Gentlemen," Milo said, "Thank you for taking time from your surgery schedules for this meeting. I have asked Angela to join us. I expect you will find our conversation compelling and must ask you to hold this discussion in confidence, as you would your medical records. You'll soon understand why. Will you agree?"

"Yes, we will," they replied in unison.

"As Angela may have told you, her dad and I worked together in Air Force intelligence's investigation and deception business during the Vietnam conflict and Khmer Rouge genocide years. Because of that background, a UN person asked me to form a covert investigative group in Bangkok. They explained their supposition that kidney transplant tourism surgeons might go upmarket as kidney prices plummeted and use their skills to perform illicit heart transplantation. Of course, this was a purely speculative theoretical concept, as there was no evidence of its happening. Still, it interested me that the UN was willing to pursue this horrible though speculative possibility. Our mission was to examine that premise, and that interested me."

"So until the *Scimitar's* photo, you had a problem on your hands, didn't you, now trying to prove a positive?" said Julian. "You decided to check out the Surgicenter covertly since we are right next door and perfect for a trial run, your test case. Maybe have a little party for the doctors; spread checkered table cloths and pour some wine; light some candles and play some 'Hotel California'; introduce Angela—the new doctor who has just moved into the PIP Tower—and launch her into the Surgicenter. You've got some nerve, Milo."

"Gentlemen, please let me finish. I formed Team Bangkok without an existing organizational chart or schematic. So, it was 'learn as you go'. When you're preparing to investigate something that may not exist, you're bound to stumble and stumble we did with regard to the Surgicenter. It looks bad in retrospect, I'll admit. For which I apologize. It's not hypothetical now after the heart-on-ice picture."

"The fact that you did it at the UN's bidding doesn't make it okay," Hu said. "Thais generally respect the UN, but the UN has no authority in Thailand. I suppose the UN has plausible deniability if your team causes embarrassing problems in pursuit of unscrupulous transplant surgeons, right?"

"Yes, as a matter of fact."

"So, what qualifies you to investigate two surgeons licensed to practice medicine in Thailand after six years of training and further examinations? We swore an oath of medical ethics, like the Hippocratic Oath that the King first administered in 1930. Angela may have explained that we are real doctors. We would never do illicit hearts."

"You have a right to be angry. I apologize," Milo said. "I'll ask our UN manager to discuss our position with the Thai authorities."

"Apology accepted, but Milo, you overstepped. You'd better get your authority straightened out before slipping into other practices."

"You are right. And it will take even more nerve to explain why I asked you to meet today."

"Okay, let's have it."

"First, about Angela. I persuaded her to join us—Team Bangkok—when she was between things. She had just lost a grant application for medical work in Thailand and had no plan B. Angela is honest and straightforward. I launched her into the Surgicenter. The moment she returned from visiting with you, she texted me, 'no hearts, impossible', and 'I am not a spy.'"

Angela picked it up, "I've felt guilty since then. You were so welcoming and professional. I saw you as real docs and was thrilled with your job offer. I am sorry about showing up under a false flag. I hope you won't hold it against me."

"We understand. You're good."

"Next," said Milo, "and here is my gall again: we want you to join Team Bangkok as part-time experts on the medical side of our investigations. Angela thinks you would be great assets to the team, given your integrity and professional expertise, your in-country insights, and foreign languages. Our UN manager agrees."

"Milo, I do admire your nerve," Julian smiled. "Thanks, we appreciate those compliments and your team's importance in this changing heart landscape. However, we have to consider something else. We are independent medical practitioners, free from facility maintenance and administrative responsibility. The Surgicenter's owners do all that and are patient and fair. We owe them our loyalty and can't allow a clandestine association to conflict with that."

"I understand, but do mull our offer over." For full disclosure, Milo told Hu and Julian that Wisut had investigated Boc and Khem after they left lunch at *Tii Baan*. "We're awaiting his report.

"Somehow, that doesn't surprise me, Milo," said Julian. "Oh, and Angela, however this relationship works out, we still want you to sign on with us."

"That's great! Thank you."

15. Opening Kimonos

Kimsan had used an iron-fist-in-velvet-glove approach to instruct Boc and Khem. His praise of their unmatched sagacity induced near-ecstatic highs for them. But Team Bangkok was a cipher, and the unspoken consequences of failure scared them shitless.

Dr. Angela Tran was clearly the key to Team Bangkok, and Kimsan advised them to follow their instincts to soften her up and gain her trust. It was easy enough for Boc and Khem to handle tainted officials and slippery business elites; they would always cave under threats of blackmail, etc. But their standard methods would hardly snare a trained spy, were Angela one, and a doctor who must have stared death in the face. They needed inspiration, so today, they strolled around the grounds of Wat Phra Kaew in search of some.

Wat Phra Kaew, located in the Royal Palace Park, is the most sacred temple in Thailand and, as such, houses the exquisite Emerald Buddha.

"If you look across the river, you see Wat Arun. That was the Emerald Buddha's first home," Khem informed Boc, glancing up from the brochure that provided this informative tidbit.

"Maybe the 'stunning abstractions' will inspire our sense of purpose," quoted Boc from his own brochure. "This is an 'ideal place for thought and inspiration', of which we need plenty. The Emerald Buddha is a 'thing of almost ineffable beauty, almost unworldly', yadda, yadda.

"I'm not much into 'ineffable,'" he said as they stood looking at an entrance to the temple. "But the Guardian Giants do speak to me."

The Guardian Giants, fearsome maces at hand, are icons of strength and security from ancient times. They stand before the temple entrances to thwart any threat to the Emerald Buddha. Green, red, blue, orange, and ocher tiles color their warlike dress and highlight their savage visages. Images of their faces with curved canines appear throughout Thailand as reminders of a mythical past.

"Look at the bastards, Khem, formidable and threatening like the old-time Mafia dons fancied themselves. Look where muscles got them: not into temples but prisons and graveyards. But we are the new guys; subtlety and smarts are sour strengths. Muscles won't get us to Dr. Tran. Brains, Khem, brains. We have to think."

"So why not set up a dinner with the docs," said Khem. "We'll tell them vaguely why we need to meet Dr. Tran and maybe open our kimonos a little. They can probably help us connect with Team Bangkok. Otherwise, we're up the creek."

That evening, Boc and Khem met the docs at the Blue Sax.

"Not a bad restaurant if you like Isaan food and a moaning saxophone," said Boc, exposing his culinary and musical opinions.

"I suppose it's a matter of taste," said Hu. "Angela says she loves the combination of spicy food and edgy jazz. So she tries to come on Wednesday nights for the improvisational 'Woodwinds Conversations' show."

"A matter of taste, as you say, Gentlemen. Let's order our drinks and talk about why I asked you to meet," said Khem.

"Tonight, Boc and I want to open our kimonos," said Boc. "Long ago, we dipped our toes into Mafia waters along the border when the Khmer Rouge were raging. We ran a few logs and sold some visas, but we've been clean bureaucrats doing the city's work since then. Recently old connections with long memories—we'll call them the Council of Elders—contacted us. They have eyes and ears everywhere, influence among important people, and a long reach that extends even into the United Nations. They believe that an 'aberrant syndicate' has set up a heart transplant facility that is responsible for the recent heart-on-ice debacle."

Khem picked up the narrative, "None of the Council's Asian syndicates are involved, but they are taking unfair blame for the horror and losing lots of money. That pisses them off. They appointed us the 'tip of the spear' in Bangkok and charged us to take out the aberrant syndicate. We've never been in the wet stuff of 'taking out' something. So, that worries us.

"But we aren't alone. According to the Council's UN asset, the UN has commissioned a group called 'Team Bangkok' to do the same. So the Council has instructed us to meet with Team Bangkok and combine resources to deal with the aberrant syndicate."

Boc added, "They also learned that Team Bangkok inserted a young doctor, a mole, into a kidney center—undoubtedly the Surgicenter's new hire. That was a huge clue. We believe she can lead us to Team Bangkok."

"That would be Dr. Angela Tran," said Hu noncommittally, "right, Julian?"

"Angela, a mole? She's not a sneaky sort. She's a Thai citizen from Ubon Ratchathani and a great doc. In fact, she's the one who will get our—your—dialysis unit up and running," Julian added.

"Nonetheless, the Council believes that Dr. Tran can lead us to her boss. Our instruction to join Team Bangkok was not just a suggestion. Our balls are on the chopping block. Failure to make contact will have consequences. We believe Dr. Tran can help us out, and we need to decide how to persuade her to do that. So, there you are."

Hu responded, "So, this Council thinks something like 'the enemy of our enemy is our friend'?"

"That's about it. We see Dr. Tran as the gatekeeper. We just need an introduction so we can talk."

"Well, Gentlemen," Julian said, "if my balls were on the chopping block, I'd introduce myself and say, 'Angela, we believe you work with a group with interests similar to ours. We would like to meet your boss and combine forces'. If she doesn't buy what you are selling, she will smile innocently and start speaking English," said Julian. "But I'd be very nice. She's a fine person and doctor, and we don't want to lose her."

"I agree," said Hu. "Being up-front is the way to go. Tell her what you told us—minus the chopping block. She will need details. So why don't you just talk with her?"

"Asking favors isn't instinctive to us; not part of our usual toolset," said Khem. "Boc and I will discuss the matter further and get back to you. In the meantime, keep this conversation private."

Julian and Hu returned to the Surgicenter and discussed Boc and Khem's revelations. It all seemed strange. They couldn't understand Boc and Khem's weird reluctance to be upfront. So, they opted to wait to hear Boc and Khem out before taking the matter further.

An hour after the dinner, Boc and Khem sat in a smoky corner of their sports bar redoubt. They avoided lubrication at times of decision, and this was one of those. As bubbles rose in their club sodas, it was a time for reflection and decision.

"The Guardian Giants inspired me again today," said Boc. "I like what they represent: protection and loyalty as sentinels to the Emerald Buddha, guarding against all threats. It heartens me that the Council considers us guardians combating modern threats.

"I admire the giants' commitment to something bigger than themselves—if you get my drift. I always leave the Wat Phra Keaw feeling more potent than when I arrived, not with greater physical strength, but inspiration and a sense of greater courage."

"What a contrast with our supposed Mafia guardians, our not-so-courageous predecessors who were ruthless and murderous and ever at war for no high purpose. That's not us today. The wet stuff is archaic, *passé* nowadays. We work at the interface where all bad is not evil, where human weakness caves to blackmail and persuasion," said Khem.

"Maybe weaknesses of our own are standing in our way with this Team Bangkok thing. The docs think we should just explain our situation and ask Angela to introduce us to her team leader. Sounds easy, so why not do that? Because it isn't instinctive? Because it isn't our accustomed way? So what, Khem?"

"I hear you, Boc. Maybe it's a matter of trust. Julian and Hu trust her; even so, she hasn't come clean with them about spying. They are still young, slightly wide-eyed. Our years have brought us closer to human nature and taught us to understand some things. Julian says Angela's parents worked the border chaos as intelligence agents when she was a child. How did a childhood in a nest of spies affect her? I would like to know the real Angela before revealing ourselves."

"Like, how would you do that, Khem?"

"Well, I know muscle is out of the question. But maybe some light pressure to soften Angela up and gain her confidence. Like a nudge, Boc, nothing really physical; just close-up, leaning into-her-space sort of thing.

"So, how's this? As Angela heads home from the Blue Sax one Wednesday night, Skinny and Horapha confront her in a pretend robbery. Skinny will apply his dead eyes and whispery voice. Horapha will go along for bulk. So, they catch her alone, pretend to rob her, and give her some goosebumps. At that moment, we'll happen to be cruising down Soi Rangnam, see the robbery in progress, swoop in for the rescue, and chase her 'assailants' into the park," said Khem.

"We'll introduce ourselves and say 'thank goodness, we just finished a meeting at the Surgicenter', or some such. We'll promise to report this incident to the authorities. Yadda, yadda, yadda. We will be heroes; we'll gain her trust and take it from there."

"Like the old assisting-a-maiden-in-distress thing, with us gallantly fighting off villains. Not a bad idea, but it will require perfect timing."

16. Peace Park Intimidation

Angela's heart beat to the rhythms of Thai jazz. When the atmosphere was right, she could hear notes rising from the Blue Sax just a few blocks down Soi Rangnam, an easy walk from the PIP Tower. The restaurant was the converted home of a former Chulalongkorn University musicologist. His son, a Thai jazz devotee, hovered nightly over a moody sax, his mellow notes an aural counterbalance to the spice of Isaan food. The occasional strike of spoons against plates punctuated the plaint of Isaan jazz crying from the nostalgic horn.

Angela had come tonight for the week's 'Woodwinds in Conversation' improvisational. She had also envisioned a plate of Laab Gai, a peppery Isaan salad, one of her favorites. Som Tam or Laab Gai, start with either one and then try something new from the lengthy menu.

Angela enjoyed eating alone. It gave her time to think. *So now it is hearts.* Her medical mind reviewed the complexities of heart surgery, its demanding operating equipment, and rare surgical teamwork. *Such a huge project should be impossible to conceal. So, how has it gone undiscovered? Like Kiet says, the prepared mind may discover things, but who could even imagine such a thing?*

Angela finished her meal, listened to the trio's final piece, and waied to the musician as she stepped out onto Soi Rangnam and turned toward home. Lost in thought, she passed a closed fruit stand and then the red lanterns of a Japanese restaurant. She passed the windows of a seafood shop, where wide-eyed fish stared from beds of ice, then by a corrugated metal door leading to who knew where, and on past Santiphap Park.

She knew the park well. She strolled along its shady paths several afternoons a week to escape Bangkok's heat and haze. She enjoyed its variety of tropical plants and the small signs identifying them. Or she would just sit, admire the fountain and enjoy its cooling spray. She and Kiet often ran here after evening workouts. It was a public park whose name meant 'Peace' in her English vocabulary. There were community exercise sessions in the early mornings—all in all, a delightful place.

Deep in thought and strolling on automatic, she failed to notice two figures emerge from the park's dark arbor until they moved close to her. She stepped quickly aside to let them pass while at the same time, a large man veered in the same direction as in a typical side-to-side sidewalk avoidance dance. But it was no dance: the big guy moved in closer and poked his finger at her chest. She grabbed it and bent it to the snapping point, "Do you want to keep that finger, fat boy?" He obviously did, crying, "Yes, yes."

His skinny partner smiled across square yellow Teeth and stared at her through empty eyes. A cigarette bobbled on his lip as he whispered, "Our kids need new shoes, honey. So, let's us just step into the park and talk about money."

"Do your mothers know you are out harassing women? Get lost and take your fat buddy with you. You get nothing from me." she sneered.

"What did you say to me?"

"Are you deaf? I said beat it!" she snarled. At 170 cm, Angela stood eye to eye with them.

A motor revved up in the distance.

Trying to recover his mojo, Skinny reached for Angela's arm, but her elbow struck him in the jaw before he could touch her. Then she cupped her palms, whapped his ears, and crashed her knee into his solar plexus, a close-in Muay Thai move.

Wide-eyed and breathless, Skinny followed his cigarette and a square tooth to the sidewalk, his face throbbing, mouth bloody, doornail deaf, puking and moaning. The big guy stood dumbfounded, holding his finger and watching his pal hurl.

"You, fat boy, scram," Angela spat. The big boy spun and hurried off with the spurious grace of a large man.

It had happened in an instant.

People were already crossing the street and gathering around Skinny, who was still down, gasping for breath. Angela flipped open her mobile to notify the authorities.

A dark Corolla worked its way through the crowd and stopped at the curb. Boc and Khem jumped out, looking seriously concerned.

"You look OK, thank goodness," Boc said to Angela. "We just got out of a meeting at the Surgicenter. Too bad it wasn't a minute or two sooner. This man is in bad shape. We're Boc and Khem, the owners."

"What a coincidence. I work at the Surgicenter; I'm Dr. Angela Tran. I've called the authorities already. This one on the sidewalk—step back—he's about to hurl again. He and a fat guy tried to rob me."

"Good that you are OK. I'll bet they won't try that again. Can we give you a ride home?"

"Thanks, I'm good."

"Well, it's nice to meet you. Maybe we can chat another time at the Surgicenter."

Angela walked to the PIP Tower. She entered and greeted the receptionist and asked, "Has anyone asked for me?"

"Not tonight," the receptionist answered.

Angela checked the lobby's exits and headed to her room. She turned on her new fan, adjusted the AC, and wandered onto the balcony, briefly considering an evening swim.

"What amateurs," she mused.

17. Concurrent Activities

The next day, after making early morning rounds, Angela regaled Julian and Hu with an account of the mugging.

"So, you took them both on?" Julian asked in amazement as Angela ended her story.

"Yep, just a couple of thugs. I told the skinny one to get lost. That disrespected him and pissed him off. So, he grabbed at me, which he probably still regrets."

"Bad mistake," laughed Julian.

"I learned it all at Kiet's Muay camp. I wonder if they found his tooth," Angela chuckled.

"You told the big guy to scram?" asked Hu incredulously.

"Yes, he was standing there, holding his finger, trying not to run away," said Angela. "I mean, these guys were amateurs. A robbery on Soi Rangnam in the early evening at dusk? 'Baby needs shoes', my ass. It doesn't make sense. The bosses had just finished a meeting at the Surgicenter and wheeled over to the curb to help. But it was all over by then."

The doctors had listened with smiles and chuckles until a mutual realization clicked. They exchanged quick glances.

"Amateurs, like you said, not thinking straight," said Hu, affecting a smile, as he turned toward the surgical suite. "Julian and I had better not keep surgery waiting."

But they kept surgery waiting and instead detoured into Julian's office.

"A meeting last night? The incredible bastards," said Julian. "How convenient; Boc and Khem showed up almost in time to foil a robbery after leaving a Surgicenter meeting that never took place. It was a setup. Boc and Khem in action!

"I've never imagined that side of them. I think it's time for a decision. We're not Hamlets, after all. I'll set up a meeting."

Dr. Hu agreed, but wondered who the heck this *farang* Hamlet was.

Meanwhile, Boc and Khem headed to the Erawan Shrine across town to seek divine assistance in their dealings with Angela Tran's group after the screwed-up robbery. That idiotic event was enough to agitate any rational spirit overseeing men's affairs. Their situation reminded them of the Erawan Hotel's problems before the Shrine was built.

Odd difficulties kept cropping up during the construction of the luxurious new Erawan hotel. Builders usually experience glitches during the construction of high-rise buildings, injuries to workmen falling from bamboo scaffolding being the most common. However, there had been others. Accounting variances, for example, and a shipment of white marble lost at sea—far too many weird incidents. Something must have agitated the building's guardian spirits. One astrologer suggested that masons had mislaid the foundation stone. Whatever the cause, an observance was required to appease the governing spirits. So the owners built a large, open-air shrine beside the hotel site at the intersection of Ratchadamri and Lumpini roads. Afterward, the hotel rose twenty-two stories without another hitch.

There was always lots of activity around the Shrine. Street vendors sold marigolds, garlands, joss sticks, candles, and small teak elephants representing Erawan, the three-headed elephant Indra rode across the heavens making weather. Visitors purchased cages of small birds and released them to make merit. Boc purchased a teak elephant, while Khem selected joss sticks and candles. Car horns blared, tuk-tuks tukked, and the Skytrain roared above. Tourists took pictures, chatted, and exclaimed about the bright golden figure with four faces, Phra Pom, the Buddhist and Hindu deity of good fortune and protection.

Within the Shrine's fenced perimeter, worshipers knelt in prayer around the statue of Phra Phrom. Nearby, the resident dancers performed in traditional costumes to classical music. Clouds of incense and fragrances from the myriad garlands permeated the air.

Boc and Khem sat on a bench and watched the worshipers' routines.

Khem had almost lost his religion during the Khmer genocide but regained some after Pol Pot's death answered his prayers. He would admit, however, to some subsequent backsliding. Today he would petition for a favorable deal with this Team Bangkok.

A monk passed through the crowd and handed Boc a brochure.

"What do you call your elephant, Boc?" teased Khem, "Erawan?"

"Of course. But seriously, Khem, I'm thinking about Phra Phrom's four faces. The monk's brochure here says they represent kindness, compassion, sympathy, and equanimity. Aren't we a little low in those areas?"

"Yeah, we need improvement; that's for sure." With that, Khem walked to the basin of holy water, rinsed his hands, and moved toward the four-faced, eight-armed Phra Phrom statue that sat on a platform beneath a peaked canopy supported by jeweled posts at the four corners. Incense smoke rose among the golden garlands.

Joining the other worshipers, he lighted his joss sticks with a candle, held them between his palms above his head, sank to his knees, and bowed to the ground several times before Phra Phrom. He then stood and followed other supplicants around the statue, praying silently. Finally, Khem placed his candle and joss sticks in the nearby sandbox, ending his observance.

Meanwhile, Boc offered up the teak elephant to Phra Phrom. Next, he stepped behind the statue and contributed a few hundred baht for the dancers to include his and Khem's names in the songs they sang while dancing and promised further support if his prayers were answered.

Back on the bench, Khem said, less than piously, "This is high-value real estate here in the middle of the city. I hope the spirits prioritize petitions arising from this particular Shrine."

"I would hope so."

Khem said, "Sending those two goons was stupid. She whipped Skinny and chased Horapha off. It was over in an instant, and where did all the pedestrians come from?"

"It was poorly executed. After our meeting at the Blue Sax, Julian and Hu probably suspect we were behind the fake robbery. We have to come clean with them. I'll call the docs and ask to set up a meeting this afternoon."

"We'll ask them to introduce us to Angela as respectable men who want to join forces against a common enemy, and then we'll ask her to introduce us to her boss. Everything upfront. Remember, as the monk said, we need to radiate kindness, compassion, sympathy, and equanimity."

"Don't overthink it, Khem; just phone them," said Boc.

Khem flipped open his mobile.

18. Allies of Necessity

After surgery, Julian and Hu caught up with Milo and Angela at *Tii Baan*.

"Milo, our two bosses—you saw them at lunch—invited us to dinner several nights ago and 'opened their kimonos,' to quote Boc's oblivious expression. They told us that they were once low-level *Pho Chao* members. But they had just been reactivated by a group of higher-ups, a Council of Elders. The Council's chairman called them 'the tip of the spear in Bangkok' and charged them to take out an aberrant Mafia heart syndicate."

Julian continued, "The council's chairman had learned about another team in Bangkok with a similar assignment and insisted Boc and Khem partner with you and work in a friends-with-a-common-enemy relationship."

"So, how did they learn about Team Bangkok?" Angela asked.

"I was about to ask that too," said Milo.

"Get this. The Council has a contact in the UN who told them!" answered Hu. "And they also—"

"Come on!" Milo interrupted almost explosively. "A Mafia group with a United Nations contact! The place leaks like a sieve. So, how do they know that we're Team Bangkok?"

"Here's your answer," said Hu. "The UN source told them that Team Bangkok had planted a female doctor in the Surgicenter as part of their investigation. Boc and Khem twigged to Angela, of course. They wanted to get to you through Angela."

Julian took up the story, "For some reason, Boc and Khem didn't ask her to introduce them to her leader. Instead, they looked for another way to elicit Angela's cooperation. We think this amateurish robbery was part of a scheme—maybe to soften her up. Almost unbelievable, right, but there you are."

"Amazing," said Angela.

"Whatever the case, this is a tipping point for us, and we want to join the team—right away."

"So this strange story has a silver lining," said Milo. "Team Bangkok has two new members. Welcome aboard! We'll put together a celebratory Isaan dinner soon. In the meantime, I'll get Wisut to join this conversation. As I said, he checked out Boc and Khem after you met for lunch here. Let's see what he's uncovered."

Suddenly, Edith Piaf's compelling "R"s pealed from Julian's mobile. The ring tone usually stirred his French soul, but this time not so much. He flipped open his phone, saw the caller's number, and covered the mouthpiece. "It's them," he whispered to the others around the table. He listened and nodded several times before clicking off. "Boc and Khem were calling from the Erawan Shrine. I suppose they were seeking divine intervention or something. They wanted to meet us at the Surgicenter this afternoon."

"Call them back, Julian, and have them meet you at *Tii Baan* instead. This should be fun," said Milo.

Fast feet scurried into *Tii Baan*. "Ah, Wisut, good that you got the message. Tell us what your guys turned up on Boc and Khem. And say hello to the Team's new members. Hu and Julian have just joined up," Milo said.

"Welcome, guys; looking forward to working with you. I've got some goodies here about Boc and Khem." Wisut filtered the high points of his research from his prodigious memory. "After your lunch, my brilliant postdocs identified Boc and Khem and trailed them through pages of documents going back years. They learned Boc and Khem are indeed bureaucrats nearing compulsory retirement, who had personally founded the Surgicenter and transferred its potential liabilities to a shell cooperation. Interestingly, they are also anonymous donors to Dow and Alec's clinic. My guys are great digital snoops, but they are good on foot too.

"They followed Boc and Khem through Lumpini Park, where they met with a Cambodian guy named Kimsan. He turns out to be the Asian Mafia Council of Elders chief. Cool, huh? My guys could get information out of a black hole!

"Back in the Pol Pot days, Boc and Khem worked along the Cambodia border, where they smuggled out a forest of logs and sold Thai visas for the price of jewels. Later on, they stepped from border life into Bangkok government positions, where they dealt in connections and executive legerdemain. They both live in lux condos off Sukhumvit Road.

"They consider themselves among a new breed of civilized and sophisticated *pho chaos* that never engage in the physical aspects of persuasion. Incidentally, their photos are not on the traffic camera at the corner. This means they don't drive the blue TopazEV, which has been bugging Kiet.

"So, tell me about my boys! Are they wonder-sleuths or what!?" exclaimed Wisut, excited by their findings. The question was rhetorical, of course, and no one responded.

Milo concluded, "So, it's believable that these 'sophisticated Mafias' could be behind Angela's faux robbery. A pathetic story, but comical in retrospect."

"Yeah, tragicomic," Angela laughed. "What dopes! Or, as you said, 'novices in physical persuasion', amateurs in the wet stuff. If you want to know about moving logs or selling visas, that's them, but physical stuff is doubtful. And yes, Wisut, your guys are wonderful sleuths."

"Thanks, Angela," Wisut continued. "Boc and Khem aren't dumb or particularly dangerous. Their peers respect them. The so-called Council of Elders deals with problems and adjudicates complaints among various Mafia syndicates in the SE Asian sphere. Boc and Khem are council members," Wisut continued. "The council tries to set a tone of civility and sophistication among the various syndicates. A Mafia metamorphosis, you might say.

"The council's chairman, Kimsan, is an important Phnom Penh banker closely related to the Sen family."

"You mean to Khun Sen, the Prime Minister of Cambodia?" asked Hu.

"One and the same," Milo said. "Kimsan ordered Boc and Khem to 'take out' the heart transplant syndicate on behalf of the Council. In their world, orders have consequences, which means Boc and Khem will be in a load of trouble if they fail. We expect them to meet with the docs imminently."

"Imminently, Milo? That soon?" Angela joked as Milo worked this translation of a *farang* word into his Thai vocabulary. Not amused that his *farang* word had flopped, he continued, "Julian and Hu will introduce Angela to Boc and Khem later today. Angela will accuse them of engineering the robbery.

"She will also tell them that we know Kimsan's niece is a loose tongue in the UN. That tidbit can hang out there as insurance," said Milo. "I'll step into the conversation when the time is right."

When Boc and Khem arrived at *Tii Baan* that afternoon, they were surprised to find Hu and Julian sitting with Angela. Recovering, however, they presented themselves politely. Angela nonetheless bullied them.

"So are your tips of a spear or common robbers?" she was haranguing them when Milo stepped in.

"Why are you being rude to these gentlemen, Angela? It's not necessary. I'm sure they have things to talk about. Isn't that true, gentlemen?"

19. Cultural Blend

In the Bangkok Office of Medical Affairs, Noi's mobile chirped. It was Angela.

"Hi Angela, I was just thinking about you. Actually about wine and dinner some night. How are you?"

"Great minds, Noi. Can't complain. In fact, I'd like to celebrate my new job! I'm officially employed at the Surgicenter. Bangkok's treating me very well. How's it going with you?"

"Life's good. I just got a new apartment near Queen Sirikit Park and the Emporium."

"Great address. Looks like the girls are doing pretty well for themselves," said Angela. "How about dinner tomorrow night?"

"Let's try the new US Steakhouse on Sukhumwit Road. It's the real thing, owned by a Canadian-American. Good bar, good beef. And they say the atmosphere is surprising. How about Saturday night?"

"Sweet. About 8:00?"

Angela arrived early at the Texas Steakhouse.

A greeting sign in artful Thai and English scripts hung beneath a pair of longhorn cattle horns. The Muay Thai rhythm of a drum, cymbal, and eerie horn played in the background, and Angela detected overtones of a Texas beat skillfully intertwined with the native sound. A hologram of the American-born King as a young man stood upon a teakwood plinth, binoculars in hand and camera across his chest, surveying the dining hall as if noting Thailand's bounty of "rice in the fields and fish in the streams." Only an artist could create this subliminal blend of two countries' culinary environments. *But, being a cultural mix myself, I'll sip my wine and admire the illusion.*

Noi found Angela's table. They exchanged greetings.

"Congratulations on the Surgicenter position."

"Thank you, Noi," Angela said, taking a breath. "First, I want to apologize for not being completely upfront about why I wanted to work at the Surgicenter. This will sound like something out of a James Bond movie, but the boss has cleared me to talk to you about it. I work with a covert United Nations outfit called Team Bangkok. We are looking into black market organ commerce and possible heart transplant tourism in the city. They had me get a job at the Surgicenter to have an inside look. Playing a spook was hugely uncomfortable. No hearts there, of course."

"I suspected you left something out of the story when you came for your license. Your Team isn't the first to eye the Surgicenter, and I can also say it is a legitimate operation. The owners—whoever they are, probably a shell corporation—touched all the cultural and religious bases and got a sense of the impoverished neighborhood dwellers before starting to build. The Medical Society believes the Surgicenter's dealings with donors are fair and scrupulously correct. Donors are never coerced. So, as you say in the US, we 'let that sleeping dog lie.'"

"Julian and Hu believe everything is on the up and up, and I do, too. However, I want to be upfront with you because I don't want to lose my Thai license. Lose it here, and it's gone in the US too."

"No worries, especially since your assignment comes through the United Nations. Furthermore, any threats to your license would have to get by me first. That won't happen."

"Thank you. That's a relief."

Their wine arrived, and they toasted to friendship and good health.

"I learned more about Dr. Hu," Noi said, "I called Professor Chin, Hu's professor, in Beijing about an administrative matter. Naturally, Hu's name came up as we talked. Professor Chin asked about Hu and told me, without reservation, that Hu exhibited remarkable talent and determination while in surgical training. Professor Chin told Dr. Hu that seriously ill patients sometimes don't make it through surgery. But if one of Hu's patients died, he would fall into a terrible funk. Professor

Chin was worried about Dr. Hu's depression after his first patient died. Hu was devastated, moody, and withdrawn. Hu believed he was being followed by his dead patient in the form of a mythical corpse called Jaingshi."

"Hu has a ghastly tattoo of Jaingshi on his chest and stencil of a Jaingshi on his shirt pocket," said Angela. "So I looked Jaingshi up. He's the mythical hopping zombie, a corpse risen after a wrongful death in a state of partial rigor mortis. He hops around because his muscles are stiff, and to make matters worse, he's coated with a revolting frosting of decayed flesh that smears on anything he touches. Yuck. He is commonly a villain in Chinese ghost stories and horror movies. It was new to me."

"The professor told me that Hu is very superstitious. He comes from a region in Thailand where the spirit world oversees daily life. In time, Hu returned to his usual intense self but still kept a *feng shui bagua* mirror outside his window to ward off Jaingshi. The professor wonders if fear of Jaingshi isn't what drives his busy perfection."

"Makes sense," Angela said, "Speaking of weird things, what about the heart-on-ice situation? Has the Medical Council looked into it?"

"The photos created a huge stir on the council. They deplore the possibility, but they're too worried about the city's hospital finances to consider much else. FifTiin of our public hospitals are on life support, and three are broke and closing. So the medical council and the city fathers are in a financial stew."

"Really?"

"Yes, but they broke out the champagne when investors purchased the defunct hospital on Ratchathewi Road. The investors say they plan to privatize it and reopen its doors—whenever."

"What about the doctors? Are they concerned about a black market operation moving in?"

"They would be, but they have about eight hundred patients each. Their backlog is their priority. The medical society understands the need for transplant capabilities in general but that it isn't financially feasible. Maybe a world-class transplant team will set up here someday. In the meantime, we work hard on prevention."

"Prevention goes a long way, but tourists could be a huge cash cow. It's a stretch to imagine a clandestine heart transplant operation in Bangkok, but we aren't so sure," Angela said. "Our team thinks the heart on ice was intended for a patient in Bangkok who is deathly ill if not already dead."

"That's horrible, that proposition." Noi paused and swirled her wine. "Change of subject: rumor has it that you were mugged the other night, even in your safe neighborhood. Thank goodness you're OK. Could it be connected to the transplant investigations?"

"Who knows? No harm done—to me at least, thank goodness. Can't say the same for the thugs," Angela laughed. "'First do no harm' doesn't apply in self-defense."

"I take it you've had training, but keep your eyes open anyhow. Now, on to more pleasant subjects. Cheers! Let's split a steak."

"Cheers!" said Angela.

20. A Failing Heart

A snippet of the haunting drum-cymbals-oboe music heard at ringside at Muay Thai bouts sounded on her phone as Angela sat glued to a microscope. Dow was calling her.

"Angela, I need your help right away." Aiming her video phone at an elderly woman, Dow continued, "This is Ms Harris. Her phone ran out of minutes, and she set out from the RFC hotel to recharge at the 7-Eleven, but she didn't get far. Ms Harris nearly collapsed at the fruit stand. An old patient of ours brought her here. She is in acute pulmonary edema.

"She says she has a cardiopathy with chronic congestive heart failure. Her doctor said her old heart needed replacing. So, she came to Thailand for a heart transplant and has waited in the RFC hotel while a local hospital prepared for her surgery.

"You can see she's dyspneic, out of breath, and anxious but not panicking because she's been in this shape before. Her neck veins are distended; she has 4+ pitting ankle edema. Her sputum is pink and frothy. I've given her Furosemide, and she is beginning to diurese. So, she's hanging in, but I think talking with a fellow American would make her more comfortable."

"Please ask if I can examine her remotely on your videophone." Ms Harris nodded permission.

"Hello, Ms Harris. I'm from America too. We are both a long way from home. What state are you from?"

"California, where it never gets this hot," she wheezed.

"I'm from Texas. It's hot there too, and just as humid. I understand your condition. Dr. Dow is taking good care of you. Do you have chest pain?"

"No, but I can barely catch my breath," Ms Harris responded.

"The Furosemide will fix that soon. Would you please let Dr. Dow hold her phone to your chest so I can listen?"

Ms Harris agreed, and Angela heard a marked tachycardia and a cardiac gallop behind the wheezy wet lung sounds of pulmonary edema.

"I know you are anxious, Ms Harris, but Dr. Dow says you are already diuresing. May I ask you a few questions that shouldn't tax you. When did you get to Bangkok?"

"About two weeks ago. I'm getting my breath back now."

"Were you this sick when you arrived?"

"Yes, and no. I've been in heart failure for a long time, but fairly stable and mobile but still fragile and needed a transplant. I was hopelessly far out on the list, so what do you do if you're old, desperate, and rich? You do anything you can do! My doctor told me I could get a transplant in Bangkok without delay. He sent me to a man in San Francisco who arranged everything. I've stayed at a hotel near here with a nurse, waiting for the hospital to call me in for the surgery. They are trying to find a suitable heart for me."

"I see," said Angela.

"I was bored to death, and my phone ran out of minutes. So I headed to the 7-Eleven down the street and nearly passed out. The nice lady sat me down in a little red chair and called the woman who brought me here. I have no idea how they got me into a tuk-tuk, for goodness sake."

"I'll bet you forgot to take your meds."

"Yes, I did. I ran out of meds, breath, and minutes, all at the same time," Ms Harris chuckled.

Angela said in Thai, "She's getting better, Dow. Do you plan to hospitalize her?"

"Yes, she's being admitted to the cardiology unit at Bangkok City-1. It's first class. They'll take good care of her."

"She'll need to be under guard, you know, and require utmost security. She's potentially explosive. Her minders are probably searching for her already."

"Don't worry about that. Monitors at the nursing station will display her EKG continuously, and a soldier will stand guard at her door. In addition, nurses will round on her hourly."

"Thanks, Noi. Please keep me posted." They ended the call. *This may be the most important case of my brief professional career.*

21. The Faux Monk Deception

The noontime sun dazzled off the ripples of the Chao Phraya River, scattering diamond traces across the green apron of City-1 Hospital's grassy embankment. A royal-yellow minivan drew up to the hospital admissions walkway. A young man, disguised as a monk clad in saffron, stepped from the passenger seat and slid open the side door. A mechanical lift delivered another saffron figure in a wheelchair to the walkway. The young imposter took gentle charge of the wheelchair and adjusted the figure's sun hat while the senior monk parked the van. The three entered the hospital.

As they made their way to Reception, the crowded space quieted, hands formed temples before each person's chest, and heads bowed. A murmur of respect, "Phra Ajaan," was heard as the crowd parted, allowing the fraudulent monks respectful passage.

They arrived at Reception and accepted the attendant's bowed head and pious high wai. Smiling benevolently, they stated the purpose of their presence. The daughter of an American Buddhist had requested a period of chanting for her ill mother, a Ms Harris. "This elderly lady is in the cardiac care area," the senior monk said. A hospital attendant stepped forward unsummoned and escorted the three to the elevators. They arrived on the cardiac floor and explained their mission to the ward manager, who directed them to a private room. A slim soldier in a tight khaki shirt, radio at his belt and a truncheon at hand, bowed his head, waied respectfully, murmured "Phra Ajaan," and stepped aside.

Ms Harris lay partially elevated in her bed, and while she looked a bit dazed, she was not overtly fighting for breath. Tubes and wires connected her to an IV stand and overhead monitors.

The visitors closed the curtains. The attendant who had joined them at Reception injected a sedative into the port of Ms Harris's

IV tubing. Sighing deeply, she drifted deeper into sleep. The younger imposter monk withdrew a first-generation smartphone and two off-the-shelf Bluetooth speakers from a compartment under the wheelchair seat. Recorded monotone chants of devotion to the mystic laws played in the small space. He then removed a second device from the compartment. An EKG tracing ran across its LED screen, and an output cable extended from it. The attendant unplugged Ms Harris's monitor and substituted the line from the device.

Just after Ms Harris' computer readout at the nurses' station suddenly flickered, it displayed a normal rate and rhythm. An astonished nurse exclaimed to no one in particular, "She's out of atrial fibrillation! Maybe the monks would also chant for some of our other patients."

The monks lifted Ms Harris gently from the bed as the chants continued, placed her into the wheelchair, and draped her in the mannequin's saffron robe. The senior monk applied makeup foundation and darkening powder to Ms Harris's pallid face, placed the sun hat on her head, and drew its brim to protect her eyes.

The mannequin sat propped to 45 degrees in Ms Harris's bed, and Ms Harris's blue beret-type surgical cap fell jauntily across its forehead and over its closed eyes.

The monks turned off the chants, placed the phone and speakers back into the wheelchair compartment, and parted the curtains to wheel their companion through. They nodded a blessing to the soldier and the nurses' station as they left. Once back in the minivan, they drove in the direction of Chao Phraya River, pier 10.

A crewman tied his vessel tightly against the dock at the pier so that the monk's wheelchair could glide aboard, and the boat set off across the river. There, the monks wheeled Ms Harris across the Saphan Taksin pier and transferred her into a blue TopazEV.

Ms Harris regained consciousness briefly, looked around, and wondered, "Is this a car from the airport?"

22. A Lady in Saffron

The monks helped Ms Harris from the TopazEV at the RFC hotel and wheeled her along the walkway that curved across the manicured green lawn into the lobby. They skirted the duty-free sections, waied to the doorman, entered an elevator, and ascended to Ms Harris's suite. Her nurse and the gentleman who had accompanied her from San Francisco awaited her.

"Welcome back," the nurse said, steadying Ms Harris from her wheelchair to the bed. "I was sorry to hear about your trouble. But, first of all, let's change those clothes. Saffron is not your color."

The gentleman smiled at this droll comment and said, "We're glad you are back from your hospital visit."

"What hospital?" Ms Harris wondered. "Oh, yes, I recall. Some of it is coming back. I remember seeing a nice doctor nearby. I knew I was in pulmonary edema. Luckily I survived this episode, but I seem to have lost a day."

"Well, they straightened things out at the hospital. Our doctors will take over your care until your surgery."

"I'm afraid I'm a bit mixed up. I recall going out to buy some minutes for my mobile, nearly passing out, and here I am back in the hotel! Hmmm, it's very confusing. However, I don't like being cooped up, and I will take a walk tomorrow," said Ms Harris.

"But you mustn't stray out of the hotel again in your condition, Ms Harris. We can wheel you around the hotel gardens instead. There is a wonderful jungle garden on the rooftop with an aviary of parrots and beautiful birds. Misting fans are everywhere to keep you cool as you enjoy the day. It's most delightful," advised her gentleman attendant.

"Thank you, but I'll manage to keep myself entertained," she said, seeming more alert. "I want some quiet time to clear my mind after these drugs wear off. I must talk with my daughter. She doesn't know I paid out a chunk of our family's savings when I scheduled the heart transplant.

"I guess I've been in denial, and today was a wake-up call. Now I'm feeling comfortably old and happy to continue along the natural course of my life wherever it takes me. I'm considering canceling the surgery. We can talk about a refund later," she said.

"Please do reconsider, Ms Harris. We'll talk more in the morning. We've already paid for your new heart and are waiting for the donor," the attendant said.

"A donor? You can't mean a human donor! I was led to believe it would be a mechanical heart," she said and reached for the headboard to steady herself.

"Ahh, Ms Harris," he took a short breath. "We should have it for you soon. In the meantime, you can wait here in comfort. But it's late now; you must be tired. We'll talk more tomorrow."

The nurse tapped a few pills from a container and poured Ms Harris a glass of water from the bedside table. "So, here's your heart medicine. Have a good night's rest."

"Yes, of course," Ms Harris responded groggily, drifting off and sinking beneath the sheets as the sedatives began to circulate.

23. Unwary Perhaps

Milo looked around at the group in amazement. "What do you mean, Ms Harris was kidnapped? Are you kidding me?" He was supremely pissed off.

"Whoa, Milo," said Angela. "This was a slick deception. Everyone was duped. Two faux monks and a fake attendant pulled it off with a mannequin and off-the-shelf electronics. The imposters played on the piety of the hospital staff and the young soldier guarding her cubicle. The ruse fooled everybody. The 'monks' rented a minivan in royal colors and used a public riverboat to escape in broad daylight. These people know their stuff."

Milo shifted from his green-beret bluster into a reasonable calm.

Changing the subject, Kiet said, "I hope they have a heart for Ms Harris."

"If they don't, they will try to get one. She's probably a million baht patient. Why else would they go to this much trouble? If a new heart is coming by air, it might lead us to the clandestine surgery hospital—if we can intercept it.

Milo continued, "Kiet, I want you at Don Muang airport tonight with a flashlight and quiet shoes. Figure out how something can be smuggled through there. Find records that haven't been filed yet: recent bills of lading, etc.—Wisut's white hats can't get at those—records especially of private flights, arriving six hours before the motorcycle accident. Also, check for manifests of goods shipments since then. You're looking for records of any package that could support a live heart in transit."

"Wisut's guys came up short on the city files, but that is right down Boc and Khem's bureaucratic alley. So I'll have them search customs and other pertinent government paperwork—arrivals, departures, overstays, etc.

"Wisut, have your team examine the RFC hotel records for guests who might have appeared sick, needed wheelchairs perhaps—not colds or vomiting or fear of farting, but enfeebled ones. Also, look for guests, who've left for a week or so, and returned later...or not at all.

"And Angela, we need to work on Hu's Jaingshi delusions. Put on your doctor's hat and work with Wisut and his psychologist. I have a feeling that we'll need Hu's expertise before long. The whole team needs to stay in action.

"Dow, Ms Harris appearing in your clinic was a stroke of luck. If anything else comes your way, let us know."

Kiet said, "For something coming our way, how about this, Milo? Near the RFC's limousine entrance, our camera picked up an electric blue TopazEV early last night. It dispatched a saffron-clad figure in a wheelchair. What do you think? Ms Harris perhaps? I told you the TopazEV was suspicious, and here it is."

"Excellent, Kiet. Another stroke of luck," Milo enthused. "Maybe they aren't so far ahead of us after all. When we untangle this heart mess, we'll wonder what took us so long. So, let's keep on it."

24. Milo's Stroke of Genius

It bubbled up from a dream in the depths of sleep: A blue TopazEV parked at the RFC. The dream jolted Milo awake. *That's it! The syndicate simply exploits the RFC's luxury transit package to move transplant patients into and out of Bangkok without arousing suspicion.* The RFC had designed the luxury package to bring customers from the airport to shop duty-free. Those exhausted by a day's exuberant shopping could stay and enjoy dinner and a night's sleep in the RFC Hotel. *But so could the syndicate's patients for even a longer stay...such as those awaiting surgery.* The syndicate would pick patients up from the hotel for surgery and return the survivors for the trip home postoperatively. The cunning was admirable; there was a beauty in this simple duplicity. Milo shook his head, berating himself briefly for having missed the obvious.

Milo texted his revelation to the team and crowed, "A slam dunk. Nothing suspicious. The RFC folks wouldn't notice the sham. And, think about it: the lady being returned from her kidnapping in the blue TopazEV, our Ms Harris, serves as our index example."

"So I have a plan," he continued the next day in the lab meeting.

"I suggest we turn Kiet into a hotel management consultant. I know the owner of the RFC—helped him foil an attempted kidnapping of his daughter—and am confident he will approve the plan. He is a fine man. He would never be involved in a black-market operation and would hate learning of this abuse. I'll speak with him later today.

"In the meantime, Kiet, I'm sorry your airport visit last night was a dead end. But shoulders back, young man! It's time to become a hotel consultant! I'll ask our game developer, Yasuhiro—he's finally back from his trek—to put together a back story and some flattering videos of you in consultation mode, the whole package."

The next day after a light workout, Kiet donned stylish business attire with polished oxfords. The name tag on his jacket's lapel read, "Khun Prasert, Guest Services Consultant". He looked distinguished as he viewed the world through clear lenses in modern Korean frames.

At Milo's request, the owner of Royal Facets Complex Ltd. had arranged for Kiet's visit to the RFC Hotel and ensured the manager's cooperation. He asked her to tour Khun Prasert through the physical plant and open the books and computer system to him, emphasizing that. Prasert will be interested in recent guests with physical or medical requirements.

When Kiet stepped into the hotel's lobby, Khun Sathit, the hotel manager, greeted him. "*Sawatdii kha*, welome to the RFC Hotel." He returned the greeting with a wai.

"I see you entered through the duty-free section," Sathit said. "You have arrived at the last stop in our seamless luxury experience. Shall we start with a tour of the facilities? Perhaps with our pool, spa, and other guest amenities?" she said within earshot of other employees.

As Khun Prasert and Khun Sathit moved across the reception area, she said softly, "Forgive the hype and formality. I know you have a serious purpose here. I will help you any way I can." She wondered what movie this 'Khun Prasert' had stepped out of.

"Thank you, Khun Sathit. My group wants me to meet Ms Harris, an American from California. She went missing for a day but has returned to the hotel," said Kiet.

"Yes, Ms Harris occupies a suite with her nurse. She arrived last evening by wheelchair and was received by her attendant, who is Asian but not Thai."

"Okay. Let's pay Ms Harris a visit. I'm good with Thai, but my English is rusty. Perhaps you will translate for me if it comes to that," said Kiet.

"Happy to," she said. "One must be conversant in English and Chinese to work in the guest services business, as, ahem, you know, as a consultant in that area," she teased. "But don't worry. Ms Harris's nurse speaks some Thai, too."

They pressed the button at Ms Harris's door. The nurse answered the chime, and the three exchanged polite wais.

Khun Sathit introduced herself as the hotel manager and Khun Prasert as the hotel's security chief. "We received a worried call from Bangkok authorities last evening, inquiring about Ms Harris. They explained that she had left the hospital. Surprised, the front desk explained she was still in the hotel with her nurse and attendant. Khun Prasert would like to have a moment with Ms Harris."

Glancing quickly at the attendant, who shifted from foot to foot, the nurse responded, "Ms Harris isn't in the apartment, poor dear. She's relaxing in the rooftop garden. She thought she would enjoy a 'perfusion of jungle plants and 'a karmic relationship with the birds.'"

Earlier, her attendant had wheeled Ms Harris into the elevator which rose to the top floor and discharged them into a small alcove leading to a heavy door into the rooftop garden.

"Thank you very much," Ms Harris said. "If you'll just bump my chair over the threshold, I'll take it from there." Once inside the garden, she gripped the wheels' handrails and rolled alone onto a packed gravel trail.

Ear-splitting screeches of parrots in high dudgeon greeted Ms Harris, heralding the wonders of life in this warm and fecund place. Flowering plants grew in lush abundance. Mangoes and jackfruit hung from trees, banana clusters grew upside down from broadleaf plants, and fruity aromas scented the air. Wooden frames buttressed the trunks of young saplings. A sense of beauty overcame her, and with it, a brief whirl of dizziness.

She backed her chair to a nearby bench and locked the wheels. Before her, branches overarching a gravel path created a tunnel in which patches of light played whimsically into the distance. Mentally, she assumed a Lotus position and proceeded to meditate.

Twitters and calls of birds and buzzing of insects surrounded her. *They are letting me know they are alive.* Gradually, her mind chatter slowed, and the garden din faded into a hum. Relaxed and mindful, she rolled her chair into the tunnel.

She breathed deeply and strained against the wheels that crunched along the infinite path. Further along, she came upon a cage of birds darting from twig to twig, and from memories of her childhood came the French poem of a bird who 'halting in her flight on limb too slight, feels it give way beneath her, yet sings, knowing she hath wings.' She raised the latch of the cage, leaned back in the chair, watched the birds take wing, and listened to them singing as they flew skyward.

Their elevator ascended to the top floor, and Kiet and Sathit stepped into the rooftop jungle. Packed gravel trails led through curated gardens, forever green. Benches sat here and there, intended for rest and meditation. Sathit and Kiet wondered which path Ms Harris had taken. They set out along one beneath overhanging branches.

Further down the verdant trail, they came upon Ms Harris's wheelchair, one wheel propping open the door of a wood-framed birdcage. Ms Harris sat slumped against the chair's canvas back, her arms hanging motionless over the sides, her face up, her eyes gazing lifelessly skyward. There was perhaps a trace of a smile. The birds had taken flight.

Kiet checked her carotids and knew that Ms Harris was dead. He wondered if Ms Harris was herself a Buddhist and made merit through the ancient practice of *fangsheng* by freeing the caged birds.

Khun Sathit called management and instructed them to notify the authorities of a death in the rooftop garden. When she and Kiet returned to Ms Harris's room, the nurse and attendant had also taken flight.

Returning to the management office, Sathit summoned the greeter who had welcomed Ms Harris to the RFC. He recalled the blue TopazEV and a monk assisting a nice lady dressed in saffron from an TopazEV into her wheelchair and into the main RFC lobby. A *farang* Asian gentleman intercepted them and took charge. Ms Harris's US passport was still among the Registration files, but there were no identification papers for her nurse or companion.

"What a morning," said Khun Sathit. "I'll check the books and interview everyone in Reception for other recent guests accompanied by a medical companion. We'll also keep a close lookout for such guests in the future. And, if there is anything else I can do for you, anytime, day or night, do let me know," she said.

"Thank you," Kiet said. "I'll stay in touch."

25. A Decrepit Hospital

The experience with Ms Harris was a turning point for the team. For good measure, Milo reconstructed the events surrounding Ms Harris's death for the rest of the team—unnecessarily, but he was the boss.

A transplant tourism organization had brought her to Bangkok and placed her in the RFC Hotel to await a compatible heart.

"A tuk-tuk brought Ms Harris to Dow's clinic after she fainted on the street attack. Dow stabilized her and transferred her to the cardiac unit in Bangkok-1 under marked security. Then, in an audacious ruse, faux monks kidnapped Ms Harris and returned her to the hotel in a blue TopazEV. She died the next day in the jungle garden atop the hotel, having released small birds from their cage into the sky.

"Khun Sathit confirmed that Ms Harris arrived from the airport via the RFC's luxury conveyance system. So far, this is our most valuable clue," Milo said and wondered, "Wouldn't it be convenient if the transplant facility were nearby?"

Angela said, "Yes, I get it, Milo. We need to investigate the decrepit hospital on Rachatewi Road. It's just a kilometer from here. I'm on it."

"Yes. So, the transplanters might be hiding in plain sight," said Milo. "Smart, huh? Do check out the hospital, Angela, unobtrusively. Other thoughts?"

"The hospital's a stroke of genius, Boss," said Kiet. "But now, about the blue TopazEV again. I'm thinking it probably handles all the syndicate's local transportation needs.

Wisut's guys say it's not registered in Thailand. So if we learn who owns it, maybe we'll have the bad guys."

"Right, Kiet. My White Hat hackers have searched thousands of vehicle documents. Think We need to figure out a way to find it. "

"Well, Khun Sathit has asked her staff to watch for the blue TopazEV. She plans to scour the hotel books for guests with medical problems. We'll want to keep that relationship open," said Kiet, smiling.

"Yes, nice to have such a smart woman helping us out," said Angela. "I'll ask her to lunch."

"We have to find the Topaz and grab the driver. He could lead us to the boss in Bangkok. Let's figure out how to do that," said Milo. "Think about it."

26. The TopazEV Hack

That night over beers at *Tii Baan*, the team members discussed how to hack the TopazEV.

Angela was first to suggest attaching a GPS to the car, following it around, learning the driver's habits, catching him unawares, and grabbing him."

Kiet elaborated that the car has to be still for us to attach a GPS. Suppose we have the drone follow the TopazEV around until it heads to a charging station. That might require some time, but the drone can loiter over the car until it heads for a charging station. Then we'll hustle there in the tuk-tuk. An electric tuk-tuk is rare enough to draw most drivers' attention, and Angela can distract him further. I'll slip a GPS under the car. How about that?"

"Not bad, Kiet, but I have an idea myself," said Milo, "Quite a brilliant one."

"Would we expect anything else?" Wisut joked.

"So, here's the ploy. Yasuhiro will build a stunning Facebook site called 'Thai TopazEV' with flashy animations of a TopazEV sports car floating in space, others whispering down Sukhumvit Road, and speeding along the Andaman coast.

"The site will announce Bangkok's first 'TopazEV Owners Club' and invite all Thailand's TopazEV owners—our suspect being the only one at the moment—as charter members of this prestigious club. They will be invited to tell about their TopazEVs, explain how to import one into Thailand, and talk about Bangkok charging stations. Suggest inviting other car enthusiasts to join the club or starting a TopazEV dealership in the Quintessence Mall—yada, yada. It will be a website for car guys, especially those with EVs in mind. We'll just wait for our guy to fall for it."

"Am I a student of human nature, or what?"

27. The Englishman's Last Ride

The presses of the Bangkok *Scimitar* revved up again. True to its commitment to sensation, today's front-page photo showcased a new Bentley G T, a paragon of exotic automobiles. The cerulean blue convertible graced the showroom in the Siam Quintessence Mall. Shoppers could browse Rolls Royces, Bentleys, Lamborghinis, BMWs, Maybachs, and other notable conveyances among the many luxuries offered for sale in this exclusive mall. Underground, below five floors of elegance, is Asia's most dazzling marine exhibit, the 360-Degree Aquarium. So, in the Quintessence Mall, visitors can go from the pinnacle of shopping delights to the depths of the blue sea. However, the accompanying news story was not a pitch for exotic cars. Instead, it was about a probable death and a body disappearing from Bangkok's luxury shopping mall in broad daylight.

The *Scimitar* article quoted the car salesman who had assisted the portly Englishman into the driver's seat: "This is a death car," the salesman said. "There's no blood on the posh leather seat, but look at the wrinkled upholstery.

"The gentleman arrived in a wheelchair accompanied by two attendants. He told me he planned to buy a Bentley convertible after his operation. He was in a jolly mood, gripping the wheel and smiling like he was already driving. I noticed his blue-rinsed hair nearly matched the shade of the Bentley's paint job and had to chuckle. He was chuckling too when he stopped breathing, looked shocked, and slumped over the steering wheel.

"I radioed an emergency to the mall's nurses," the salesman continued, "lifted the poor fellow out of the car and began CPR. No luck, a feeble pulse, if any, I wasn't sure. Security blocked off the scene with rolling screens, and we waited for the ambulance to arrive. His attendants appeared and loaded him into his wheelchair. They assured me that they would take care of him.

"It's hard to remember the exact details. The ambulance people arrived a few minutes later and had no idea who the other first responders were. The ambulance driver radioed the hospital, who had no idea either, and the police also had no idea...truly a mysterious disappearance."

The newspaper story continued: "Shoppers come to the Quintessence Mall to dream dreams, not confront mortality. Nonetheless, they were drawn to the Englishman's apparent death scene as word spread throughout the mall. The titillated crowd stood around the showroom, murmuring and speculating even after the man's disappearance.

"Then, according to onlookers, a wild-eyed man dressed in an Alpine outfit—boots and wool socks, hydration pack upon his back—suddenly appeared from the direction of the sports department and elbowed his way onto the scene.

"Wielding an ice ax over his head, he shouted in an agitated voice, 'I was out climbing, so I didn't do it!' Surprised onlookers gave him space. In Thailand, winter sports are rarer even than winter itself," the paper observed.

"When security tried to intervene, the man holstered his ax, darted away, and retreated down the stairs to the 360-Degree Aquarium. The security officers and some people from the crowd raced at his heels. Security officers said he positioned himself in the center of the 360-degree glass-wall tunnel through the aquarium's depths. It was a strange scene, this wild-eyed man waving his ice ax around, as leopard sharks and other fish glided unperturbed above and on either side of him, while colorful sea creatures flittered among the reefs and kelp."

The article concluded, "He continued his threats, once feigning a strike to the aquarium wall. 'I'll flood the place; I mean it" Averse to a flood of legendary proportions, security officers eventually talked him down, promising him the Bentley if he would come along with them. He is currently resting in the psychiatric ward of Bangkok City-1."

When Milo read about the Englishman's death, he almost blew a gasket. "Here we go again," he sputtered. "Another missing person, possibly a dead one this time. He planned to buy a Bentley after his operation. I'll bet he was waiting for a new heart. So, who took the body? And what do you do with a corpse on your hands?"

"In Bangkok, you cremate it," answered Kiet, who had come into *Tii Baan* for coffee. "But I doubt you can just drive by and leave a body off at a crematorium, even in a Bentley."

"Kiet, as a legal matter, can a corpse be burned without proper papers?" Angela asked, having arrived in time to hear Milo's outburst.

"I'll put Boc and Khem on it," said Milo. "Check hospital and police reports, visa records, and local crematoria. And, speaking of Boc and Khem, there is another matter," continued Milo. "It's about Dr. Hu."

"Boc and Khem really like Dr. Hu. They trust him and think he's brilliant. But Boc says they are worried. Apparently, Hu seems withdrawn, nervous, and easily annoyed. Julian reports that Hu spends too much time with his VR system and too little in the OR. That could cost the Surgicenter a bundle. They want to know what's going on with him."

Angela said, "Julian and I worry about Hu's personality changes. The scrub nurses speculate that Hu's Jaingshi might be re-emerging. If Boc and Khem have noticed something odd, we must help Hu. It's time to get together and consider how we can."

Wisut, Angela, Kiet, Julian, and Milo met that evening and agreed that Malcolm Bren, the computational neuropsychologist, and Yasuhiro Tanaka, the fantasy game creator, should contribute their talents to the planning.

"Malcolm and I have discussed using virtual reality for treating mental disorders," Wisut said. "Hu's case might be a good first one to treat, given his interests."

As the meeting commenced, Kiet's mobile buzzed. It was Wanarak, Kiet's old friend. "Kiet, I've just let some tourists off at the Chinatown dock. As they were leaving, some guys pulled up in a blue TopazEV, like the one you told me about. They popped the 'frunk' and unloaded something large. I swear, it looks like a body bag. They dragged it to a long-tail boat idling beside the pier and humped it in. You may have caught a break, Kiet. Come on down."

"I'm on the way, thanks." Kiet clicked off. "Wanarak called from the Chinatown pier. He's spotted a body bag heaved from a blue TopazEV into a long-tail boat. Sorry guys, we'll have to postpone until tomorrow. Come on, Angela."

Kiet and Angela hung on as the electric tuk-tuk tore off into the night, weaving through the traffic. The pier's floorboards rattled as the tuk-tuk bumped onto the Chinatown pier. Wanarak was waiting.

The TopazEV was gone, and the long tail boat bearing the body bag was already getting away. Wanarak's boat was idling, and Wanarak was itching for a chase. They jumped aboard, and after an underwater burble, the engine roared, and they shot off in pursuit.

"Hold on to your heads!" shouted Wanarak as his boat fixed like a stinger missile on the other long tail and accelerated in pursuit.

Night traffic on the Chao Phraya is an infinitely varying game of dodge-the-other boat. There are no traffic lanes. So, in addition to the two long tail boats racing across the river, brightly lighted hotel and dinner boats moseyed along, tour boats chugged back and forth, ferries worked from dock-to-dock, and cross-river traffic headed to seafood restaurants. Within this haphazard traffic, heavy-laden barges—strung together six or eight in line—lumbered along behind tugs in the middle of the river. A fast chase in this traffic required sharp eyes, fast reflexes, and a cool hand on the tiller. But for river rats such as Wanarak, this was no problem.

Unfortunately, before Wanarak could work his way around the last barge, the other boat had sped ahead of the barges and ducked into one of Bangkok's network of canals. The chase was over. Wanarak had lost.

"No luck tonight," said Angela. "If that body bag was headed for disposal, the syndicate's crematorium is across the river. We have to find it."

"Wanarak, you did great. Thanks. It was a close call. I know you are disappointed, but we'll get them next time," said Kiet.

"And there probably will be another *next time*, sorry to say," said Angela. "These creeps still don't have their shit together, if you'll pardon the English, so we can expect more body bags."

Always upbeat, Kiet said, "Wanarak, we'll want to book a river tour with you when we're done with the bad guys."

"Any time," said Wanarak. "I'll take you to the Wat Arun, the Temple of Dawn. You can climb to the top so Angela can look across the river at the Royal Palace Complex and Wat Phra Kaew, 'laid out in all their majesty' as we tour guides say. Angela also needs to see the Royal Barges Museum before the next barge procession. Awesome!"

28. A Cyber Exorcism?

Wisut opened the meeting the next day to consider relieving Hu of the Jaingshi delusion.

"Angela, Kiet, better luck next time. The other guy had a head start. But you think the syndicate's secret crematorium is across the river?"

"Yes, and we're on it," said Kiet. "We plan to..."

"So, we're here to figure out how we can help Hu," Wisut interrupted obliviously. "We agree that this Jaingshi delusion is driving Hu's deterioration. We've assumed that Hu wears a Jaingshi tattoo on his chest as gallows humor, maybe to lessen the stresses of his job. But it has to be more than that.

"Hu's struggles—his irritability and reluctance to operate, for example—are worsening. His scrub nurse, Mina, thinks Hu actually saw Jaingshi in the OR one night, which freaked him out.

"Angela says that Dr. Noi spoke with Dr. Hu's Chinese Professor, Dr. Min, about an administrative matter. As the call ended, the professor asked about Hu's work and mentioned the Jaingshi obsession. He said Jaingshi first appeared to Hu after a patient died on the OR table. Professor Min assured Hu that a pulmonary embolism caused the patient's death, definitely not a surgical error. He thought Hu had put the delusion to rest and was sorry to learn that it had recurred.

"What about Professor Min's hypothesis, Malcolm?" Wisut continued. Could the stress of a surgical death cause Dr. Hu's Jaingshi delusions? Could this be something like PTSD that some soldiers experience after wartime traumas?"

"Possibly analogous. Hu's condition does have some hallmarks of PTSD. For instance, Jaingshi appeared after harrowing emotional trauma—a battle against death on the operating table—and Jaingshi has intruded unbidden repeatedly.

"Hu's is not a degenerative disease, genetic disorder, or a tumor that a neurosurgeon could pluck out. It's a whole-brain disruption, as

PTSD probably is. Imagine a disorder involving about eighty billion neurons and their many connections. You never find causative lesions at autopsy. So Hu's Jaingshi delusion will be hard to treat," Malcolm said.

"No lesion? So, what's the cause?" asked Kiet.

"To use the medical word, it's idiopathic, of undetermined cause. Sure, there must be an underlying process that doesn't appear on tests. Today, some basic scientists believe that neurochemical abnormalities in the Hypothalamus-Pituitary-Adrenal axis— the HPA axis—might be involved. These abnormalities could cause deregulation of the brain areas involved in emotion, memory, and reflex survival behaviors," lectured Malcolm. "Some workers think that sub-microscopic-synaptic crosstalk or intrusive reverberating circuits rejigger normal brain activity, resulting in an episode."

"That's some heavy stuff, Malcolm," said Angela. "This static and biochemical cascade among so many synaptic connections is ill-defined, right? You are saying it's a paroxysmal disorder without a focus."

"Yes, sorry. I got carried away with too much basic science gobbledygook."

"Yet somehow Jaingshi pops up, a full-grown zombie when the chemistry is bad, or there's a short circuit?" said Kiet, astounded. "So, an obscure cause with no treatment?"

"Definitely obscure. So only non-specific treatments are recommended: rest, self-care, and counseling; perhaps some tranquilizers and antidepressants. Electro-shock therapy may occasionally help depress intrusive thoughts and suicidal ideation, though I don't recommend it."

"Do your own studies of consciousness have anything to offer?" asked Julian.

"Sorry, Julian, they don't. So far, I've only done computer-brain interface experiments with volunteers. They wear a mesh cap that supports an array of micro neural sensors—experiments being the operative word. So far, the setup has generated suggestive but poorly reproducible whole-brain interactions. Nevertheless, we've seen some glimmers of success and believe it will be useful in treating patients who suffer from whole brain and paroxysmal disorders."

"So, the mesh cap array is off the table," Angela said, "but the wait-and-see approach or a few antidepressants aren't good answers either. In my opinion, we should..."

Wisut interrupted, "Like I said, I have some ideas. Suppose we could eliminate the static? We could digitally harmonize and reset the abnormal microcircuit that triggers a Jaingshi event. We'd be performing a cyber exorcism, so to speak.

"Here is my thinking," Wisut continued, his excitement building. "Yasuhiro has combed Chinese literature and sketched Jaingshi. Our postdocs have developed a 3-D video from the sketch, showing Jaingshi in action. Take a look."

"He is a scary dude, don't turn the lights off!" Julian laughed. "But it shouldn't be hard to run away, as clumsy as Jangshi is."

"But he just keeps on coming," laughed Yasuhiro, "You can run, but you can't hide!"

Gazing upward as if transported, Wisut proposed, "Suppose we use Yasuhiro's visuals to build a Jaingshi-like zombie-bot and incorporate it into one of Hu's Virtual Reality surgical programs and give it animation.

"Picture this: Hu's working along in a VR heart procedure when our Jaingshi bot pops out of a parallel reality and says something like, 'Yeah, it's me, the real Jaingshi, Hu, and not the pseudo-zombie that's been freaking you out. It's an apparition that harasses you. But, it's illusory, Hu. I'm the real Jaingshi. So, let the illusion go'. And voila, Hu is cured," Wisut concluded, spreading his arms as if enraptured.

"Poof, Hu's delusions are gone. Wow, what a great academic experience! My postdocs will love it."

"Whoa, Wisut. Try to quell your academic excitement," Angela said while Wisut paused for a breath, "but you didn't listen to Malcolm's words. Jaingshi symbolizes neurological and psychological things that we don't understand.

"My god, Wisut, cyber exorcism is a catchy pseudo-scifi scenario, but—"

"So, guys," began Wisut, "Here's the issue—"

"Whoa, I'm still speaking," said Angela. "The issue here is *not* the excitement of the cyber world. It's how to treat Hu's psychological problem. You and your guys are imaginative, but the two physicians here say, 'first, do no harm'. You guys have no idea what condition you propose to treat and what adverse effects your attempts might have. Your 'cyber exorcism' is experimentation. It has never been done before and probably never even imagined."

"But—"

"But, remember, Dr. Hu's a real person. Hu is not a 3-D game piece or a circuit out of harmony. He's our friend," said Angela. "Wisut, after hearing your fanciful concept, most doctors would wonder just who's in need of treatment.

"No cyber exorcism for our friend. Instead, I propose," Angela said, "that we encourage Hu to see a Shaman upcountry near his parents where he grew up. It may sound fanciful to us, but Shamans still appeal to the spirits of people who live there. They still cure maladies, reset outcomes, and cast out demons."

Kiet smiled and nodded, "Let's talk to Hu."

"I'll buy that," said Wisut, with Malcolm nodding agreement. "Why didn't we think of that? Nevermind."

The next day, Angela, Julian, Kiet, and Hu's scrub nurse, Mina, sat down with Hu and explained their thoughts.

Hu broke into tears.

29. The End of Jaingshi

Dewdrops glistened on jungle leaves as Hu and his elderly parents trod the worn path to the Shaman's simple teak house. A young boy opened the door to them. All was dark within save a smoldering fire in the center of the room. The Shaman sat motionless by the firepit as a thin trail of smoke coiled to the ceiling vent. On a rock beside him lay a ball of moist clay about the size of a golden mango. A short pipette protruded from the clay. On an altar-like structure nearby were emollients, a soda bottle containing a dark potion, a tube of blood from a black dog, and a thin knife whose blade curved to a fine point. Across from the Shaman lay a white pillow for the comfort of the guiding spirit whom the Shaman would evoke. A heavy smell of spices permeated the moist air.

Hu's usual steely-eyed appearance had softened remarkably. He took a seat on the floor to the Shaman's left. Some minutes passed before the Shaman began to murmur in ancient Chinese, moving his head in rhythm. He grasped Hu's hand and massaged an emollient on its palm, back surfaces, and around the fingers. He lifted the knife and pricked the tip of Hu's forefinger. A drop of blood appeared. The Shaman withdrew the pipette from the ball of clay and placed its tip into the drop of blood and then into the vial of dog's blood, and spilled the mix onto the ball of clay.

Putting the tube aside, the Shaman kneaded the clay into a miniature human form with gossamer streaks of Hu's blood on its surface. This was Hu's avatar. The shaman then drank from the soda bottle, passed the bottle to Hu, and began his monotone chant again.

The Shaman continued chanting, nodding his head with the steady beat. Abruptly he fell silent, and an amorphous cloud gathered above the white pillow and settled there. Features appeared to shimmer across its front. The Shaman resumed the chant, his eyes closed and his chant increasing in tempo.

The amorphous being, the guiding spirit, arose from the pillow and extended a pseudopod against Hu's clay avatar to animate it. Then it hovered over the Jaingshi tattoo, ripped it from the avatar's chest, and cast it into the fire pit. Hu screamed in pain as sparks burst skyward from the embers, sweeping Jaingshi up with them. Jaingshi was gone forever.

Hu collapsed backward. The Shaman cried out, collapsed also, and began jerking from involuntary muscle contractions. The windows and door flew open and banged against the sides of the house as the guiding spirit departed.

The boy assisted Hu to his feet and escorted him out. The Shaman lay still as though asleep.

"He is gone!" Hu cried out. "Jaingshi is gone!"

30. The Crematorium

The team welcomed Hu back, freed of the crippling Jaingshi delusion. They all team reveled in the success. Mina even skipped the wai and hugged the returning surgical master. Boc slapped Hu on the back. They enjoyed Thai beer and an Isaan meal.

"You are back! Wonderful," Mina enthused. "Patients are waiting, but no surgery tomorrow after tonight's celebrations."

"Any other renovations besides me?" Hu grinned. Everybody enjoyed seeing him so relaxed and happy.

"Yes, now that you are back and Jaingshi has long gone, the renovations are complete. Patients from France are already scheduled for the Hu-Debois team," said Julian, "right Mina?"

"Our reputation spreads."

Milo turned serious, "The team has made good progress in your absence." He told Hu about Wanarack's pursuit of a suspicious long tail boat carrying a body bag to a presumed covert crematorium."

Kiet nearly bounced from his chair. "But the next day, we took Wanarak's longtail up the klong that the other boat had ducked into. We spotted a squat, windowless brick building with a pier and loading dock. It looked suspicious, so we tied up to investigate. Modern crematoria don't emit smoke or odor, so we launched the drone in infrared mode. It flashed a heat signal. Without a doubt, we found the covert crematorium!"

"The drone got a heat signal. How cool is that!" Angela joked.

"Great find, Kiet!" said Hu. "So that's where the syndicate disposes of their failed surgeries."

"Most likely, and there's more," Milo said. "An excited TopazEV owner—the only one in Bangkok—responded to our Thai TopazEV page. He regrets he won't have time for club activities for a few months.

"Wisut's guys traced his URL to a computer in the Burmese Embassy. So, Kiet flew his drone over the embassy, revealing a blue TopazEV parked in the drive. So, the drone scored twice this week!" said Milo. "The driver is a Burmese person named Muang Saw."

"We have to meet Saw," Kiet said.

"Yes, we also need to learn more about Burma," said Angela. "We know that the Junta renamed Burma to Myanmar a few years ago, pasting a new label on the same rotten can, and they hate Aung San Suu Kyi and her Nobel Prize because they fear democracy. That's all I know."

Kiet said, "Some Burmese ex-pats describe being forever whipsawed between Suu Kyi's arrests and subsequent releases. The junta's fear that democracy might catch fire always starts another atrocity. It seems to go back and forth like vicious clockwork. Suu Kyi's released from house arrest now and making speeches again, so be ready for the next calamity."

"Can't the US or somebody do something about Burma?" Julian asked.

"Unfortunately, the Iraq war overshadows the current Burmese situation. Kiet's ex-pats are right. My UN contact says even the monks are dangerously pissed off, and the junta is rumbling; rioting could erupt any time," said Milo. "Then there is the ongoing ethnic minority situation."

As the conversation about Burma stretched on, Khem and Boc exchanged glances. Khem's foot almost jiggled out of his flip-flop. "Remember, guys," Khem said. "Don't forget we have access to the movers and shakers in Burma."

"How so?" asked Angela.

"Through our friend, Kimsan. His bank in Phnom Penh does business with the banks in Rangoon and, therefore, has access to Burma's elites. Kimsan says there's lots of dirty money to wash in Burma, and he runs their main laundry. He promised us help, and we could use it now. I'll contact him."

"Do it," said Milo. "And we'll snare our TopazEV driver. I think we can flip him, and we'll have a spy in the Burmese Embassy."

Ever realistic, Angela asked, "How do we snare him, and why do you think Saw will flip?"

"We'll figure out how to catch Saw and tell him he's the lowest man in a dangerous syndicate, meaning he is disposable and will be the first to go when the shit hits the fan, which it will. If Saw hasn't figured that out yet, we'll help him understand," said Milo, his eyes flashing.

30. Angela to Phnom Penh

Apart from Skype conversations, Angela had last seen her dad after finishing Kiet's training camp. Now that she had settled back in Thailand, it was time to visit him again.

Amid the rush and hubbub when she first landed in Bangkok, Angela had overlooked the subtle touches that made the Suvarnabhumi airport unique, such as how jungle gardens and traces of old Siam softened the shopping mall atmosphere. Amazing how this wonderful airport had arisen from a cobra swamp during a time of political upheaval in Thailand.

She was particularly interested in the airport's signature statue of Vasuki, the colorful three-headed Serpent King, the Naga, from Hindu and Buddhist mythology. The huge sculpture portrays mighty warriors tugging Vasuki's head and tail to and fro around a central spool to churn the Milk Ocean into the legendary nectar of immortality.

Angela wondered wryly if clever designers intentionally placed this statue in the Departures Lounge as a *double entendre*. She smiled to herself. *I'll welcome a draught of that nectar when I'm on the way out.* For now, Angela enjoyed the sweet nectar of youth, and her permanent departure was a lifetime away, while Phnom Penh was only an hour by air.

Air travel always excited Angela. Suspended above the world, she meditated upon her fluid future until the wheels touched down in Phnom Penh International. Her father was waiting for her at the gate. After their years of separation, they greeted each other with long hugs. "Angela, you're looking so good. Bangkok obviously agrees with you."

"It sure does, Dad, and you're looking mighty sharp yourself. Retirement must agree with you — if retirement it really is. You are in such demand, and on two continents! Tell me about your offers."

"There's lots to tell. The tribunals are dragging on as they wind down, but my job is over. So let's go catch up at the Tonle Sunset Bar. During the earlier active days, we translators called Tonle Sunset the 'Bar of Babel' where we untangled our tongues after hours in the Tribunals."

"Bar of Babel — where you guys babbled, very cool, Dad. Leave it to you linguists to tangle things up. I remember you talking about it and am excited to see it finally."

They negotiated a tuk-tuk ride at the curbside, headed into the city, and arrived at the three-story Franco-Asian building that housed the Tonle Sunset Bar and Restaurant. Its polished teak stairs reminded Angela of Boc and Khem's log-smuggling stories.

The rooftop tables were also teak, and the walls the ubiquitous Asian yellow. Angela and her dad ordered shrimp and baguettes and raised wine glasses to one another. Monks strolled along the river walk below, their robes blending saffron into the sunset's display.

"This restaurant was always busy during the Khmer Rouge Tribunal days. We'd all kick back with a baguette and beer as the polyglot murmurs of lawyers, diplomats, journalists, spies, and wannabes hummed around you.

"Mr. Smith, our polyglot chameleon of the Ratchathani days, showed up once in the role of a French diplomat. I had to avoid him, thinking he might expose my scrubbed identity. So here today and gone tomorrow, that's Mr. Smith. Do you remember him?"

"Sure, Dad, I could never forget him. He gave me the nested dolls on my sixteenth birthday. As to your scrubbed persona, I imagine morphing from a clandestine intelligence operative to translator spook was fairly easy."

After Colonel Tran's retirement, Air Force Intelligence removed *spy* from his résumé, recast him as a professor of Asian studies and simultaneous translator, and inserted him into the translation staff of the Khmer Rouge Tribunals.

"A slam-dunk for this old spy. So now, tell me how you and Team Bangkok are getting along."

"Really well, Dad. I got my Thai medical license. The team has gelled: we've added two new members and developed a reasonable narrative about the transport of patients and, ugh, hearts. We're only a single country away from cracking things open."

"One country away?"

"Yes, our charter restricts our operations to Thailand. However, we think the heart reservoir is in Burma. So we want to learn something about Burma that we can exploit from a distance. We need a quick course on today's Burma."

"A quick course on Burma? By a great coincidence, I know, the Burmese expert, Edna Cowling, *the* Edna Cowling. Edna has, in fact, asked me to consult on a thriller she intends to write about the Golden Triangle and the infamous Opium King, Khun Sa.

"I met Edna first – it seems like yesterday — when she arrived in Phnom Penh as a chronicler supporting the US staff at the Tribunals in about 1998. Over time, she became infuriated that only three persons were found guilty of crimes against humanity. So pissed off, in fact, that she took up her pen to do battle with evil and, falling upon the outrageous brutality of Burma's military, she recently produced her historical account of the Junta's battles against democracy and Suu Kyi.

"Somehow, Edna knew I had kept up with Golden Triangle affairs during the Ubon days when Sa was moving tons of heroin – so much heroin they said that every addict in America would shake if Sa died. He traded opium for guns to his huge personal militia, so we just monitored him and kept out of his way."

"Dad, you're digressing."

"Okay, okay. This bit of history dates me, but I'll bet Edna will be pleased to fill the team in on relevant aspects of Burma. Let me email her and introduce you."

"Please do, Dad, right away. You're awesome: Air Force Colonel, spy, linguist, translator, and connector of people."

"Thanks, Angela. I'm happy to help out. This heart thing is nasty business. Phnom Penh papers are pushing a *Chao pho* connection. We've always lived in benign symbiosis with the Mafia, but now we worry."

"Same in Bangkok. But the team knows the local Mafia isn't involved because we work with two *Chao pho* Elders who are sullied by all this."

"Strange bedfellows, your team and the Mafia, but you may need them. Always good to have access to the darker side. We learned that in the Pol Pot days."

"As to those days, Dad. I want to ask you about something that has percolated in my mind for the years since."

"Well, now."

"Remember how you and Mom had missions along the Cambodian border? I want to ask you about a particular one you, Mom, and Milo made with Mr. Smith. It was just before my sixteenth birthday. Mom picked up a package from the medical commissary, and off you went. I hoped you were headed to Bangkok for a birthday present for me. Instead, you came back excited, laughing, and high-fiving—but no present. Pol Pot died in his sleep on that birthday. People say he died from a heart attack—*auspiciously*, as you might have joked. I have some questions."

"Hit me."

"What was in Mom's package?"

"Some medicine."

"For whom?"

"Uh, Mr. Smith, and ultimately for Ta Mok, who had asked for some heart medicine that Pol Pot needed."

"Did Pot die from a heart attack?" Angela asked.

"Pot died in his sleep, they say."

"From a heart attack?"

"Possibly, possibly not. I'm not a doctor."

"But Mom was. What did she think?"

"She seemed to think not."

"Is that why all of you were smiling and fist-bumping that day?"

"Yes."

"Milo said details will come out in 30-odd years. Do I still need to wait to know the truth?"

"Obviously not, my dear daughter."

"Thanks, Dad. I'm so proud of you and Mom. I almost can't bear it."

"We are beyond proud of you, too."

"Dad, do we still need to keep our eyes open?"

"Yes, even today. We worry about long memories."

31. The Charging Station Scam

When Angela returned from Phnom Penh, she headed to *Tii Baan* and up the rickety stairs to the computer lab. She found Kiet fulminating as he watched the video display from his drone feed loitering above the Burmese embassy. "The bastards are firing rifles at our drone right in the middle of Bangkok! We're not in Rangoon, you douchebags. Good luck taking us down without a shotgun.

"By the way, how was your trip, Angela?"

"I had a nice trip, and I'm glad to be back. Thanks for asking. Dad gave me an important contact."

On Kiet's display, activities in the embassy courtyard changed. A heavyset man with slicked-back hair was getting into the TopazEV. A guard swung open the embassy's heavy gate for Saw and moved into the perpetual mob of protesters. The crowd carried banners demanding, "Stop ethnic cleansing! Listen to The Lady! Save the Rohingya." They jeered but grudgingly made way as the TopazEV proceeded into their midst. Newspapers said protesters swarmed the American and European embassies on weekends with the same messages.

Security thugs followed the car into the street and muscled it into the crowd. They appeared thick and stubby from the drone's vantage point, wearing swamp-green uniforms and berets. They bored into the protesters, swinging batons at their shins.

"Nasty guys," said Kiet, curling his lip. "Look at the medals on their uniforms. Probably awarded for courageous actions in massacres of unarmed peasants."

"Bad guys. But Kiet, isn't this what we've waited for?"

"Yes, definitely. Saw's going to get the TopazEV charged. Tell Dow."

They raced off in the tuk-tuk. When they pulled up to the charging station, Saw was having a leisurely smoke, apparently glued to the entertainment display while his car charged up. He didn't notice the tuk-tuk until Angela plugged it in.

Saw suddenly gawked open-mouthed; whether it was the electric tuk-tuk or the young woman plugging in the charging cable that caught his eye was immaterial. He flung the TopazEV's door open, flicked his cigarette away, and exclaimed, "Is that an electric tuk-tuk?"

"You bet. My friend converted an ordinary tuk-tuk to an electric one," Angela said, pointing to Kiet, who was moving about and tinkering in the tuk-tuk's motor compartment. "You've got an electric car there, so why not an electric tuk-tuk?"

"Makes sense," agreed Saw.

A ragged beggar cradling her baby and several older children rose abruptly from a bench nearby and hurried toward Saw. She shoved the baby into Saw's face and pleaded, "My baby is skin and bones, and my children are starving. Please, you look like a fine man. Won't you please help, please?"

Saw knew that criminal syndicates in Bangkok sheltered homeless women, furnished them babies to serve as sympathetic props, and put the women to work begging. Saw raised his arms defensively and scolded her, "Get that baby out of my face. Go away, go away, and keep these dratted urchins off me." The older children were swarming around him, brushing and bumping him. He batted at them to shoo them off, and they left the nasty man.

Escaping from further annoyance, Saw hurried to unplug his car and got in. He slammed the door, and the TopazEV screeched away. The older kid handed Dow the nasty man's phone. They packed themselves into the tuk-tuk, grinning and laughing.

"Good job, all of you!" Kiet said as they returned to *Tii Baan* and wheeled into the courtyard. They were totally psyched and still jittery with excitement. "I can't wait to see Wisut's reaction," Kiet said. They called him right away and left a message. About an hour later, Wisut bounced into the lab. "What fun. I wish I'd been there to see the action," he said. There was great excitement when Kiet and Dow presented him with Saw's mobile. Keys chattered in the background as the postdocs downloaded the phone's data to the team server.

"This opens mega possibilities for us," a postdoc said. They scanned Saw's past movements and made plans to listen to his calls, map his routes throughout the city in real-time, and locate him at any moment. They would also have access to the EV's software, too!

They inserted a bit of software to turn on Saw's camera and microphone at their command. Saw was theirs.

"He frequently visits the Royal Facets Complex," said Kiet browsing the data. "And from there, he usually heads to the Ratchatewi hospital."

"Was he at the Quintessence Mall the day of the Englishman's apparent death?" Angela asked.

"Yes, he was," answered Wisut, inspecting Saw's trips. "And at the Chinatown pier, too, on the night of the longtail chase. Sorry to say he's been there several times since. He stays at the Riverview Hotel most nights with a mistress, I assume, but I haven't surveilled those moments."

"His evening calls to his mistress should make interesting listening," Kiet commented.

"Kiet, surely you know listening to other peoples' conversations is rude!" said Angela, in mock reproof.

"When do we start?" replied Kiet and Wisut almost together.

Wisut exclaimed, "Kiet, Dow, you and the little pick-pockets hit gold!"

In this moment of celebration, however, a harsh reality struck. "We won't be hearing anything after Saw notices his phone is missing," said Kiet. "He'll get a new one, and our opportunities will disappear. So we've got to get this phone back to Saw without arousing suspicions."

They considered and rejected several possibilities until Kiet suggested flying the drone into the Embassy compound that night and dropping the phone by the car door. Saw would think the phone had just fallen from his pocket.

"It worked," Kiet said the next morning as he preened around the lab. "We did it without rousing the security guard."

32. Edna Cowling's Consultation

True to his word Colonel Tran introduced Edna Cowling to Angela and Milo. The professor agreed to brief the team on current conditions in Burma in their historical context. She mentioned that the 'heart-on-ice' affair had become something of a scandal even in the Austin papers.

Angela soon welcomed the professor on a video call, "We're excited to have you with us, Professor Cowling. Even the postdocs have deserted their monitors to join the session."

"Thanks, Angela. I appreciate your invitation and understand how difficult it is to get postdocs away from their machines. And please call me Edna," the professor responded in her Texas accent. "Angela has asked me to give you a useful picture of today's Burma. But, first, let me say that Team Bangkok's working narrative concerning the origin of donor hearts seems credible."

Edna slipped into academic mode. She explained that the Burmese military regime was a fearlessly cohesive and all-powerful elite that held an unbreakable dominance over every corner of the country. Only the junta's paranoid fear of democracy exceeded its corruption and brutality.

As an example, Edna cited the Depayin Massacre, when elements of the Burmese army set upon Aung San Suu Kyi's entourage en route to a lecture on democracy. At least 70 people were killed, and only good fortune and her driver's quick action prevented Suu Kyi's assassination.

Then, chuckling, Edna digressed to describe the opulent wedding of Thandar Shwe, the daughter of Senior General and Head of State Than Shwe, as an example of the elite's privilege. "It was perhaps the world's most outrageous wedding that year. A gaggle of elites, who wished to remain elite, supported the celebration to the tune of fifty-million dollars, much of the extravagance encircling Thandar's neck, dripping from her ears, and hanging from her wrists—in addition, of course, to family gifts.

"However, no amount of silk and jewelry could disguise Thandar's unfortunate resemblance to her mesomorphic dad," Edna said. "Check out the online videos. See how her plump good health and that of the well-nourished attendees contrast with the skinny frames and sunken eyes of impoverished citizens on the streets of Burma.

"In fact, growing privations caused thousands of monks to take to the streets, their massive uprising now known as the 'saffron revolt'. My book describes examples of malice and corruption that maintain the chasm between the regime and a peoples' democracy."

The Professor continued, "Happily, the world is taking notice. For example, the United States Congress has recently passed the Burmese Gem Act, which bans the importation of Burmese gems. The measure is designed to deny the government income that would otherwise support repression and violence. But, unfortunately, this well-intended act has caused the price of rubies and other precious stones to soar tenfold, leading to similar increases in smuggling profits."

"Hardly shocking," remarked Wisut. "A diminishing supply of goods typically leads to increased prices. What about jade?"

"The jade trade is mainly with China and unaffected by international rates," Edna replied. "Although its abundance in the Kachin State is a blessing of riches, it's a curse in environmental destruction and death. You can find videos of massive equipment scooping away mountainsides rich in jade, leaving denuded slopes. Destitute villagers scavenge the slopes for the shards they sell to hold their wretched lives together. Unfortunately, landslides often sweep them to their deaths in pits below. Jade is a dangerous business from mining to sale.

Shifting gears, the Professor moved on to drug smuggling. "Drug smuggling is in Burma's DNA, so to speak," she began. "Even today, elephants bearing drugs and gems sway along jungle paths en route to the Thai border. From there, illicit items pass through greased hands onward. If you are wondering, old-time smugglers still occasionally use the 'condom-in-the-colon' trick for drugs.

"Interestingly," she continued, "the synthetic drugs, fentanyl and methamphetamine—'yaba'—have replaced heroin as the universal drugs of choice. They are easy to make, easy to ship, and have no growing season. So, billions of pills and tons of powder pour across the world from Burmese labs along the China border."

Wisut interjected, "Yaba and fentanyl in addition to heroin, you say. So the bad guys diversify their product lines in response to economic incentives."

Edna nodded, "And don't forget that teak logs still float into illicit commerce. The Irrawaddy River is more than just Kipling's Road to Mandalay."

Edna explained that money laundering follows large-scale smuggling and that Cambodian banks digitally transform illicit Burmese kyats into honest dollars. But, in the process, the military elite always takes a bite. "Real estate, for example, offers great laundering opportunities."

"I suppose in Burma, it's who you know that counts and who you don't know can be dangerous," said Milo.

"Very true. I list some of the names of the older generation and their young inheritors in my book. But many other power figures remain strategically anonymous.

"Finally," Edna concluded, "Burma's awful shame is ethnic crime, most recently involving the Rohingya Muslim community of the Rakhine State along the Bengali coast. The military has orchestrated bloody Buddhist-Muslim conflicts, burned villages, and massacred their inhabitants to drive them out of the country.

"Videos and newspaper photos show waves of Rohingya fleeing to Bangladesh through mud and jungle, dragging their kids and whatever belongings they can carry. Others have set out in rickety boats and drowned or been captured and sold into slavery. This all has stirred international accusations of crimes against humanity. So, I agree that the Rohingya or other minority could be a source of stolen hearts."

Snapping her fingers, Edna added, "One more thing! A hospital has recently gone up in Burma's new capital, Naypyidaw, in the shadow of the golden Uppatasanti pagoda. You might want to look into their surgical activities."

"Brilliant, Edna," said Milo.

"Thanks, Milo. I've probably gone on far too long. But one parting thought: the Burmese elites are secretive and deceitful; they are masters of subterfuge and misdirection. I wouldn't be surprised if this heart thing was created as a horrible distraction from something bigger. Just saying..."

"Thanks, Professor," Wisut responded. "We need to consider that angle."

"Also, I would advise you to keep your UN channels open for rumors about happenings along Burma's eastern border with China's Yunnan province," Edna said.

"Absolutely," replied Milo. "We will. For us all, thank you for your time. Visiting with you has been interesting, informative, and fun."

"You're welcome. Remember, beware of subterfuge and distraction'. Bye, now."

As the call ended, the team looked at one another. "Burma is a formidable opponent," Wisut said. "We need to proceed with caution."

33. Hu Presents in China

Delivered of the horrid Jaingshi delusion, Hu returned from his home village with a new sense of confidence and purpose. The transplant team put the Siam Surgicenter back on a robust and profitable course. Julian's caseload of general surgery and laparoscopic procedures increased as news of Angela's exemplary pre-and-post op patient care attracted more specialist physicians. They served more patients. Khem and Boc were delighted with their medical enterprise and increased their contributions to the local monastery and, still anonymously, to Dow and Alec's free clinic.

Hu's hours developing his Virtual Reality ideas with the Chinese company SinoAI resulted in a peer-reviewed journal article entitled *Participatory Surgical Virtual Reality Pertaining to Cardiac Procedures.* This led to an invitation to present the keynote address at the International Congress of Digital Surgery.

This year's Congress took place in the Metro Convention Center located in the new Chinese technology city near the Great Wall, some seventy kilometers from Beijing's smog. From his hotel window, Hu could see a short stretch of the Great Wall that began on the shores of the Yellow Sea and ran across the landscape for thousands of miles westward to Jiayu Pass. The Great Wall symbolized the Chinese knack for building great things to Hu's reckoning. That penchant now extended into the digital realms of Artificial Intelligence and Virtual Reality. Hu looked forward to his presentation: he and the SinoAI team had achieved more than he had ever hoped.

The next day, as the audience of experienced surgeons settled into their chairs, the chairman introduced Dr. Hu and set the timer. Hu began, "Good morning, everyone. What a great day for us all, here beside China's Great Wall. Have you walked on it yet?

It's amazing. Yet, I'm sure we surgeons recall another great wall, the wall of trainees' shoulders that we had to look over to watch a master surgeon perform his magic. As our training advanced, the chief surgeon allowed us to assist, saying, 'Retract this! Suction here! A monkey could do better than that!' and the like. As novices, that's how our long march to surgical competence began. Now, we are fully trained surgeons.

"Today's surgical residents have training assets that we never imagined. For example, they can use virtual reality headsets to watch experts perform difficult procedures, see tricks of the trade, and get the feeling of almost being there. Thankfully, VR has relegated the old wall of shoulders to the past.

"That's a wonderful thing, isn't it. What more could we want?" Hu asked the audience.

"We'd most like to participate!" he exclaimed after a pause. "To operate on a virtual patient in a virtual copy of our own operating room. Sino AI's calls such realistic immersion 'Participatory Virtual Reality'. Remarkably that is now possible."

The audience stirred and murmured. Finally, Hu held his palms up and said, "I know. It's hard for me to wrap my head around it too. But first of all, the system is non-invasive, meaning no depth electrodes, no chips. And no cumbersome VR headset across your face. Instead, the Sino AV system uses a mesh cap of hundreds of micro-neuro sensors that establish a machine-brain interface. This interface allows the software to interact symbiotically and collaborate with the resources of your own inner world of experience and knowledge, including your medical-surgical know-how. It recruits your own brain to create an enhanced reality in which you perform procedures.

"You find yourself using your own instruments in your own virtual operating room. You'll feel their weight and balance; feel the vibration of bipolar cautery; hear the slurp of suction and the swish of scissors; and so on. As the operating surgeon, you are in full control. With this package, you are not just watching a master perform surgery; you are training new muscle memory and surgical knowledge. You learn by doing. As a result, you leave the OR a better surgeon.

"SinoAI's neural nets have made this possible. In the deep learning process, they have digested staggering numbers of surgical procedures and learned the optimal techniques for operative procedures. Moreover, the system knows the technical errors that all the great surgeons have made and will automatically alert you if you make one. When that happens, you can back up and try again. If that's not enough, you can call in the original surgical procedure—it runs transparently in parallel with you. In addition, the system has trained on vast volumes of medical texts and can respond verbally to your questions. Finally, you can save a copy of your surgery to the SinoAI cloud for review anytime."

Hands shot up, and Dr. Hu engaged his audience until the yellow light began to blink. He invited everyone to visit SinoAI's booth in the exhibit hall and ended with, "A SinoAI neuroscientist and VR engineer will be there to explain the system's technicalities in terms we doctors understand."

Air conditioning kept the Exhibition Hall frigid, and the noise of a few hundred excited attendees made normal conversation almost impossible. About 80 booths exhibited computer-based surgical instruments, operating microscopes, endoscopes, and the like, all very expensive. Packed with curious physicians, SinoAI's booth, however, became the focal point of the Exhibition Hall.

To Hu's delight, Dr. Harold Stone, a Professor of Surgery at Harvard's Massachusetts General Hospital, dropped by to try out the mesh cap and AI package. A SinoAI colleague helped translate Stone's English for Hu.

Dr. Stone congratulated Hu on his presentation and deemed his paper 'important, foundational'. He thought the SinoAI system should support robotic vascular surgery and suggested collaborating to develop an AI-based surgical robot with his own company in Boston. "After all, robotic hands work with invariable accuracy and never tire," he said. "But they always need guidance such as your system could provide."

Hu thanked Dr. Stone for his compliment and expressed enthusiasm for the idea. "Let me send you a SinoAI package, and you send me a video of you performing your Tetralogy of Fallot procedure and permission to convert it to Interactive VR."

"It's a deal," Dr. Stone said.

A crush of surgeons in diverse specialties visited Hu's exhibit for the next hour. The last surgeon was Dr. Win Tung Oo, a tall Burmese surgeon with a brilliant smile and an engaging if fidgety manner. Dr. Oo spoke Thai well as he had grown up along the Thai-Burmese border, where ghosts and spirits explained the inexplicable and oversaw daily life. He and Dr. Hu had this in common.

"Please call me Wen or Oo. 'Wen Tung Oo' is a mouthful for most non-Burmese people."

"Thank you, Dr. Oo," said Dr. Hu, "I'm Hu."

Dr. Oo peppered Dr. Hu with questions. Finally, he invited Hu to visit his hospital in Burma's new capital, Naypyidaw, to demonstrate his system. "After all, it's only an hour by air from Bangkok to Naypyidaw. I'll order the SinoAI package as soon as I can clear it with the hospital's parsimonious, kyat-pinching administrator."

The gentleman accompanying Dr. Oo winced, and Dr. Oo introduced him as that same administrator.

Dr. Oo said he had trained in general surgery and done a one-year vascular fellowship at Khon Kaen University in Thailand. He said he was Burma's only heart surgeon.

Incredible! Hu thought, *one year of training for cardiac surgery. Incredible! Good that Oo plans to use our system.*

"Let's stay in touch after you order the SinoAI VR package," Hu said and added Dr. Oo's card to the stack he had collected.

Hu ended his successful day by having tea with his Beijing professor, who had attended the Congress specifically to hear Hu's lecture.

The SinoAI computer engineers raised their glasses and celebrated a possible collaboration with Dr. Stone. "Imagine, Professor Stone of Harvard University, Mass Robotics Inc, and The Massachusettes General Hospital!"

Later that evening, Hu's thoughts returned to Dr. Oo. *Strange bird, partially trained Burmese surgeon and doing hearts. Hmm.*

Back in Bangkok, Hu described how the surgeons, mystified initially by his transformative report, had besieged the SinoAI booth for details and reality checks. Then Dr. Stone from Harvard dropped by the booth and Hu's Chinese professor later. Even a Bangkok hospital's chief of surgery had invited Hu for lunch sometime soon.

However, Hu had saved the best for last. He opened his wallet, withdrew a business card, and, flicking it with his thumb, said, "Have a look at this. It's from a partially trained heart surgeon in Burma. What do you think?" Hu asked.

As the implications sank in, a stunned silence prevailed. Hu mused aloud, "Is this only a coincidence?"

"If not a coincidence," Milo said, "it will be a *quantum leap* of good fortune. But, we have to be certain Dr. Oo is the villain."

"We will create a plan to learn if it is so," said Hu."

34. A Swollen Body Bag

After an afternoon of romance in the fabled Riverview Hotel, a light dinner on the patio overlooking the river, and a couple of drinks, everything was fine with Saw as he stepped smartly from the hotel.

His TopazEV awaited him beneath the porte-cochere, AC blasting. The valet waied formally to the freshly groomed gentleman with an unusual accent and a scent of cologne. Of course, a generous tip was in order after this fine afternoon.

"*This was your day!*" Saw told himself as he settled into the TopazEV. He opened the classic blue pack, withdrew and ignited a Gauloises, inhaled the smoke from its Turkish and Syrian blend, and allowed it to drift slowly from his nose and mouth. "*I shouldn't smoke in the car, but wow, the nicotine hit!*" And drove away.

Two electric motorcycles glided out into the lane behind him.

"He just left," Angela said into her throat microphone. Angela wore a black half-helmet strapped beneath her chin, a black round-neck tank top, matching jeans, and big boots reaching above her slim ankles. Next to her rode a lean young man whose golden face showed below dark green glasses. The postdocs radioed that Saw was heading toward Ratchathewi Road. Angela and Kiet followed Saw, prepared to kick butt.

Milo watched the TopazEV bump into the hospital's entrance, drive past the main building, turn, and park by the loading dock. Saw stepped out, flicked the Gauloises stub to the walkway, and ground it beneath his foot. He whistled a tune and executed a snappy soft shoe as he headed toward the entrance.

Dressed in black, Milo was invisible in the shadows until he stepped out and poked Saw hard in the right kidney with a length of bamboo.

"Wake the guard up. We are going in," Milo ordered.

"What the ...?" Saw's smile vanished. "This is private property," he protested. "Who the hell are you?"

"You don't want to know". The former Green Beret's tone brooked no debate.

Prodded by Milo's bamboo, the guard jolted to attention and, stumbling from his chair, said, "Yes, Sir," to Milo's command and opened the heavy door.

When Kiet and Angela whirred up astride their formidable machines, Saw gaped at them slack-jawed. Kiet relieved the guard of his radio and pistol, pulled his arms backward around a pole, and flex-cuffed them.

"Saw your last bout," the guard gasped. "I'm sorry you lost that championship."

"Always nice to meet a fan," Kiet said. "Relax, buddy. Nobody's getting hurt. Stay cool and quiet, and you'll walk away a thousand baht richer." The guard looked happier, but Kiet could feel him trembling.

From the outside, the hospital looked dilapidated, scabby paint flaking from the walls, a sad victim of neglect, its grounds overgrown with weeds. Yet, stepping through the door and flipping the switch, the four entered a cleanroom meant for shoes, masks, and gowns. They then passed through swinging doors into a gleaming hall with four immaculate glass-walled rooms and the pervasive hospital smell of disinfectant. The ward was silent.

Three rooms were outfitted with typical hospital furnishings—an electric bed, vital sign monitors, IV poles, and rolling bedside tables. The fourth was disheveled, with sheets balled up in a rollaway cart, the bed askew, and an IV bag hanging off a pole, its tubing dragging the floor. Clearly, a patient had been recently discharged. "Saw, were you coming to clean up this room?" asked Angela.

"Yes," Saw replied, shaken.

"Anything else, Saw?"

"Ah, to pick up a package."

The computer monitors at a nurses station blinked silently as the group passed and turned into an intersecting hall. Finally, they arrived at a sign reading "Surgical Staff Only" on a set of metal doors that opened automatically into the surgical wing.

The operating room was clearly dedicated to heart surgery. An operating table and instrument table were grouped together with a heart pump and anesthesia machine. "You guys seeing this!?" said Angela. They next stepped into the Recovery Room, where a line of gurneys stood, and monitoring devices blinked.

Further down the hall, they encountered the stainless steel door of a cold storage room.

"Why don't we have a look in there, Saw?" Milo inquired.

"Nothing to see there," said Saw.

"Just a quick look," Milo said as he tugged the door open. A cool mist poured out. Through the haze, they saw a bench across the room and upon it a body bag. The bag bulged tellingly, and rivulets of condensation trickled down its sides.

"Oops, is that body bag the package you came for? Maybe to drop off at the Chinatown pier?"

"Uh," said Saw, glancing sidewise and shifting on his feet.

Kiet seized Saw by the back of his neck, propelled him into the room, and pushed the door closed with a woompf. Saw soon cried out and slammed against the closed door, unable to find the emergency latch in the freezing darkness.

Milo opened the door, and Saw stumbled into the hall, shivering and gasping, his face ghostly white and his lips blue. He struggled not to vomit.

"Have a seat, Saw, and tell us why you are really here."

"How do you know my name? What do you want?" responded Saw.

"We also know your wife's and kids' names—and your mistress's. What do we want? We want you to be our secret friend. We want you to tell us things we need to know, things you'd never tell anyone else. And always have your phone with you."

"Why would I do that?"

"Yeah, why would he do that?" repeated Kiet incredulously, winking at Angela. "Why, to avoid the application of other frightful measures: Long hours growing numb in the cold room, for one thing, and ...how should I phrase it? Painful bodily injury," he said, helping Saw understand.

"It's good to avoid these things," said Angela. "Cooperation helps with that."

"Let me answer before you ask, Saw. Yes, we are threatening you," Milo said. "We are being nice now, but you should fear us mightily. So, here is our take: We know you are on the bottom of the food chain in a dangerous enterprise and so expendable; you are a gofer with a nice car to drive around, doing what you're told. The bosses may seem nice now, but you will be the first to go when things turn to shit...as they soon will. We can liberate you from all that. But you have to be on our team; you have to be our man in the embassy," said Milo.

"I think I understand," replied Saw. "But I'd be in danger. These are very bad guys. What do I get for spying for you?"

"No more cold rooms and plenty of Thai Baht, depending on your output. Also, when the syndicate goes down, we will protect you and provide identity changes for you and your family. So you won't have to go back to Burma," promised Milo.

"We know that the transplant tourism operation is run out of the Burmese Embassy, probably disguised as a cultural section and operating independently of the official political activities. So you are nodding that this is true?"

"Yes."

"And my immediate assumption is that you were coming here to make up that room and pick up the body," prodded Milo.

"Yes, and yes," answered Saw.

"So, leave your 'delivery' in the cold room until we tell you to move it. Get us the names of the Bangkok boss and his partners in Burma, the company surgeon, the doctor they recruit in the West, and who brings the patients to Bangkok. Details, Saw, we want details. Who is the mastermind? Who's the money, man?"

"Most of that is above my pay grade."

"We will stay in close contact. Leave the body bag in the cold room and make some excuse to the boat captain. Clean up the room and go. Don't get caught."

As they left, Kiet cut the cuffs from the guard, gave him a friendly clap on the shoulder, and returned his radio and pistol without the clip. "Oh, and here is a thousand Baht note for your help and silence," Kiet said. "This never happened."

"What didn't happen?" the security guard said, half-smiling.

Milo disappeared into the shadows. Two motorcycles whirred out onto Soi Ratchatewi.

35. Preliminary Bot Work

After making post-op rounds, Julian, Hu, and Angela got together for morning coffee in the Surgicenter's break room.

"So, Hu, I think your VR work improves your surgery. I've never seen you do a neater anastomosis," said Julian. "It was really a great job. Angela, you should watch our videos. You'd get a kick out of the surgical skills in our little Surgicenter."

"I do watch them," said Angela. "I saw you retrieve a kidney, Julian. Nicely done, too, Doctor. You guys are probably the best in town."

"Speaking of video, I've got some news," said Dr. Hu. "Dr. Oo has made good on his invitation. The hospital director released the money for the VR system and started the paperwork. Dr. Oo wants me to demo the system at his hospital during the purchase process. That's a typical request, and we have a demo version for such occasions. He'll send the hospital plane for us."

"Wonderful, Hu," said Angela. "I'm sure you'll want to bring Julian and me along to assist you, right?"

"Of course," Hu said. "Oo's hospital has a DHC-3 Otter on loan from a Tatmadaw general. It's a short-takeoff-and landing plane. The plot says it can land almost anywhere. He flies the general even into the mountainous Mogok gemstone region. The hospital will send it to pick us up.

We have to be 99% certain that he's the guy who harvests the hearts or transplants them and not an ego-driven surgeon who thinks heart surgery is cool. So, we'll want to get a sense if Dr. Oo is that kind of guy. Without that, we can't do the deep VR fake. So, let's chat him up, flatter him, joke around, and draw him out as much as possible. And try to get the nurses' impressions of Dr. OO and get a look at past surgery records."

"Julian and I might drift around the hospital during your demonstration, learn its layout and get a sense if things aren't just right. I'll talk with OR personnel," Angela said.

"Good, we've seen you draw people out," Hu said.

"Dr. Oo's sending the hospital plane for us. It can carry anything you can get through the door, so there will be room for our demo system. But, first, we'll want to check out its storage space," said Julian.

"Better than pizza-delivery bikes for donor hearts, eh Julian?" said Hu, smiling.

"But careful with the term 'donor' when there's no free will in the giving," Julian replied.

When they were together again later that evening, Wisut asked Hu, "So, what's the story? Are we going with the zombie fake or what?"

"Probably," responded Hu. "It's a go if we're ninety-nine percent certain that Dr. Oo's the bad guy. We'll have a better idea after the visit. Are your prodigies up to creating the fake scenario?"

"Yes," Wisut replied, clearing his throat. "We use the basic modules from your aborted digital exorcism to quickly customize the deep fake."

"Thank goodness Angela talked you guys out of that exorcism notion."

"I agree," said Wisut. "Now, let's get back to the zombie-bots—you are thinking of more than one, right?"

"Yes, and they have to be almost indistinguishable from human beings with real emotions and personalities, right Wisut?" said Julian.

"Of course, our challenge will be making them clever and interactive. The bots will be Dr. Oo's burden like Jaingshi was for Hu. Ordinary deep fakes with digital voices and photos are no problem anymore. But our zombie-bots must act autonomously. Our AI can't create the subtleties and nuances we will need, so I've asked Malcolm for help. He believes his latest microelectrode sensor cap will establish a machine-brain interface and recruit Oo's brain to interact with the zombie. That should solve the potential subtlety/nuance problem. He's working this out with SinoAI's help."

"Makes sense," Julian nodded as if he weren't bewildered.

"So, if I understand correctly, we're talking about an AI-brain interaction, a symbiosis, that will make our zombie-bots as relentlessly real as Jaingshi was to me," said Hu.

"Yes. Through a machine-brain interface."

"I know your AI has trained on medical literature, but we can provide examples of doctors' behaviors, chit-chat with colleagues, discussions on rounds, and the like."

"Wonderful. We'll need as much authenticity as possible. This is a significant innovation, and my post-docs will love building the zombie-bots," said Wisut. "Can you tell me who the avatars should be?"

"Let's use a 'donor' and a 'recipient' that we think Oo murdered," Julian suggested. "Perhaps a Rohingya donor and the friendly British gent in the cold room."

"Brilliant!" exclaimed Wisut. "I'll need you to tell me when they should appear during the operation. Oo grew up in an environment of myth and magic. So, he's probably susceptible to weirdness."

"If we are certain Oo's the guy, it's a go."

36. Lengthen the Leash

Milo sent their UN manager an encrypted note: "We are dealing with an unusual Mafia-like syndicate whose actions, we believe, constitute crimes against humanity. However, our current authority to investigate, report, and disrupt is insufficient. Without crossing borders and physical persuasion, we cannot proceed beyond analysis and reporting. Our current assignment confines us to Thailand, but the syndicate's activity is centered in Burma and perhaps China. Having this knowledge without the authority to act on it is disappointing. Team Bangkok would like a longer leash."

The manager's answer arrived within twenty-four hours: "As a reminder, the precise wording of your charge is 'when possible, quietly disrupt'. We understand your operations have often been ad hoc and imaginative, and we commend your success while on a 'leash'. However, active measures involving physical persuasion are absolutely off-limits. Your geographical boundaries are fixed. But amid these restrictions, you have been subtle and effective so far. Keep it up."

The team chafed at their restrictions. Having come so far, they felt entitled to more tools at hand and a broader field of action. But the UN response was crystal clear, and Team Bangkok would have to suck it up.

Although highly irritated herself, Angela was annoyed by the general grumbling among the team members. "We aren't babies, you know," she said. "Despite disappointment, we signed a contract and are bound to its requirements. So, let's take pride in our successes. We've been 'subtle and effective' and have accomplished a lot. Our trail has taken us from a small restaurant on Soi Rangnam to the covert Ratchathewi heart surgery suite. So, let's smile and suck it up."

"Don't forget their corpse disposal route to a covert crematorium across the river," Kiet added, "Also, we've flipped Saw; so, we've got an ear in the Burmese embassy. We'll have the boss soon."

"We helped Hu get his demon exorcised; we've expanded the team; we are in tight with the medical society's Dr. Noi," added Wisut, revving up.

As the atmosphere grew upbeat, Kiet said their sophisticated Mafia allies, Boc and Khem, who were in the restaurant below, might extend their range beyond Thailand's borders.

"Yes, of course," Angela continued. "And Edna Cowling briefed us on Burma and pointed us to a hospital in Nypayitaw to investigate. We are suspicious of its surgeon Dr. Oo. In addition, Wisut and his postdocs have helped at every turn and are currently creating AI applications."

"So, we have done big things," said Milo. "And, Wisut's AI applications will arguably make our leash irrelevant."

Milo went downstairs and joined Boc and Khem, who ruminated over a beer. Milo asked, "So, what do you men think?"

"First of all," answered Khem, "I know our attempt on Angela was old-fashioned and crude and mainly my fault. But I still believe a little hands-on stuff sometimes helps." Boc nodded in agreement.

"Yep," said Milo, "The Team can't be as forceful as I'd like. There was a day when I wasn't so tractable. I've never liked being hemmed in. But, for us now, rules are rules. Did you intend to conform totally to our boundaries when you came to work with our team?"

"For the most part, but..." Khem answered. Boc nodded.

"Have you heard anything from Kimsan lately?"

"No, but we've planned to check in with him."

"Wouldn't this be a good time for that?"

"Yes."

37. Boc and Khem to Phnom Penh

When their Thai Airlines flight landed at Phnom Penh International, a young man welcomed Boc and Khem with a cardboard panel bearing their names. He collected their overnight bags and led them through sweltering heat to a Mercedes Maybach whose tailpipe steam indicated its 12-cylinder twin-turbo engine was breathing easily and its AC working at full blast.

Their driver detoured the burgeoning downtown construction zones, and the sedan conveyed them effortlessly southwest to the Sihanoukville coast. There, jungle green encroached from one side of the road and the seaside sand from the other. They entered the Oceanfront Casino Hotel's underground garage, where a private elevator lifted them to Kimsan's suite. Its furnishings were modern, and its tinted floor-to-ceiling windows provided a panoramic view of the sand and sea below. A cantilevered semilunar pool hung outside along the window section, thirty floors above the beach and waves. Submerged seats beneath its blue surface invited relaxation, pleasure, and contemplation.

A Chinese attendant saw to their luggage and inquired in formal Cambodian as to their taste for a drink or snack. Khem responded, "Perhaps later; thank you."

Kimsan strode off the elevator and greeted them with a wai and a smile. He caught the attendant's eye and said, "Scotch, a double, on ice, thank you," which inspired Boc and Khem to request the same. "Well, gentlemen," Kimsan smiled, "How do you like this place?"

"It's stunning," replied Khem. "Do mermaids come with the pool?"

Kimsan smiled, "If you like, it can be arranged. Remember, you are not guests here because the entire complex belongs to our Council associates, including you two. Sihanoukville[1] is the prime vacation spot in Cambodia and a site of international investment, money laundering, and anonymity. It's my occasional home away from home.

"My bank handles most real estate transactions and, incidentally, owns the land up to the Chinese airfield. So no worries; the booms you hear are jets breaking the sound barrier. It's all part of the Chinese belt and road program and their claims to the South China Sea.

"Now, down to business and some important things. By the way, nobody is listening in. The place is swept every morning and evening, your phones too when you arrived."

"That's reassuring," Khem said, "because a lot has happened since our walk in Lumpini Park. But, first, your niece was right to alert you about Team Bangkok."

"Yes, she's had an awesome ear for the real skinny since childhood," Kimsan chuckled.

Khem continued, "Team Bangkok is a clever group, as we were embarrassed to learn from their secret recording of our talks in the park. The Team works out of a computer lab above an ordinary open-air restaurant next to our Surgicenter.

"They have already discovered most of what the Council needs to know about the aberrant syndicate, but their charge restricts their operations to Bangkok.

"Last week, they requested authority to go beyond Thailand. Their UN manager nixed their request to lengthen their leash. So, they can only investigate and report while waiting for someone else to act."

"And the UN won't act because they lack enforcement power," Boc griped. "The UN will consider the Team's issues in committee after committee until they dawdle them to death, while this heart syndicate goes deeper underground."

"Ah, Khem, don't beat up on the UN too much," said Kimsan. "Dawdling is endemic in large organizations. Even our Council of Elders is occasionally slow to resolve conflicts among our members. But

---

1.   https://www.skyscrapercenter.com/city/sihanoukville

in the case of the UN, I wouldn't worry too much. At some point, they will pass the heavy stuff over to Interpol, take credit for solving the illicit heart trade, and get it off their plates."

"Kimsan continued, "So, I take it the Team's recent successes and vision of ongoing opportunities prompted the request for a longer leash?"

"Exactly, Kimsan. Let me update you on the team's successes. They found the hospital where the transplants are done; learned the details of transporting recipients; discovered the secret crematorium for disposal of surgical misadventures; identified the Burmese Embassy as the nidus of syndicate operations in Bangkok; and placed an ear there to gather information.

"And something else important: A fidgety Burmese surgeon, a Dr. Oo, strode up to Hu's booth at the surgery meeting in China and introduced himself as Burma's only cardiac surgeon. He raved about the VR application and ordered the full package.

"What's more, Dr. Oo invited Hu and his assistants to demonstrate the software and is sending a DHC-3 Otter to fly them up for the demo," said Boc. "They intend to get a sense of *the real* Doctor, of Oo's character, during the visit."

"So, let's assume the docs expose Dr. Oo, and their 'ear' identifies the Bangkok boss. But the big boss in Burma will remain beyond their reach. Is that about it?" asked Kimsan.

"Exactly," said Khem.

"No worries, gentlemen. My resources extend into Burma," said Kimsan, "and I'm prepared to deploy them for the team on behalf of the Council of Elders."

"We appreciate that," said Khem.

"A plane, you say?" said Kimsan, glancing at his watch. "I hate to break off, but I've got a meeting right now. We'll get together again in the morning. I have some ideas that might be useful.

"So, gentlemen, stroll along the beach this evening if you like. But don't set foot into the jungle green which spreads to the highway; cobras spread with it. Also, beware of the green felted casino tables. They'll try to bite you in the wallet. Our cashier has a roll of chips for each of you. Enjoy it. Have a nice dinner and have fun!" said Kimsan as he hurried toward the elevator.

"Wonderful...and the mermaids?" smiled Khem.

"They like the moonlight," said Kimsan.

"Oh," Kimsan paused, "you'll see Chinese everywhere. They are important tourists and large investors. In fact, many of our Elders want peer triads to join our SE Asia groups. But that can wait until tomorrow. Ah, but the moon is rising," Kimsan smiled, glancing out the window as the elevator door closed.

At breakfast the next day, Kimsan cocked his head to the side inquiringly and said, "You gentlemen certainly look no worse for wear."

"No hangovers for us," said Boc. "We restrained our appetites for food and drink, what with mermaids and a rising moon."

"Glad to hear that you didn't rein in your appetites for everything," said Kimsan. "So let's get down to business. This morning I have two things on my agenda.

"I'm impressed with Team Bangkok's management of their end of things. But they can't get to the Burmese prime mover because of the UN restrictions, right?" said Kimsan.

"Yes, precisely," said Khem. "Because of their geographical restrictions. And regarding physical persuasion, the cold room is as far as they can go."

"Which is, of course, why you are here. As to expanded geographical range, my bank provides laundry and investment relations for Rangoon's main bank. So, we understand each other and have some mutual trust," said Kimsan. "For example, it's almost impossible for individuals to move large amounts of Burmese Kyats internationally, so we often wash the darker reserves of our Burmese investors.

"For instance, our Rangoon branch recently purchased a stolen title to a tract of teak forest worth easily a billion Kyats—roughly one million USD—for 500,000 USD from a certain general. Our Singapore branch sold the title for 1,000,000 USD on the international market to Chinese investors. So, our bank walked with $500,000, and the general is happy with his cut, and so are we. So, don't worry. I'll put my finger on your 'money bags.'"

"Remarkable, Kimsan," said Khem. "We also wanted to mention...."

"Sorry for that little non sequitur, Khem, but let me go on," said Kimsan. "I mentioned that a thought struck me last night. Like your boy Wisut, I couldn't figure out a business plan that would support something as big as this heart thing. Then somebody— Edna, didn't you say?— spoke of the Burmese penchant for deception. Then you mentioned a general's airplane on loan to the Naypyidaw hospital. At breakfast this morning, I brought that to Zhang, the leader of our Chinese friends' Triad."

"And?" Boc and Khem said almost in unison.

"Okay, okay," said Kimsan, enjoying his build-up. "Zhang thinks the hearts are actually a deception. Our Chinese friends live on the porous border with the Burmese Shan and Wa provinces. So they know smuggling when they see it. And after the US sanctions, gem prices are going through the roof, so Zhang appreciates your information and will take action. If I understand the Triad, there may be blood as red as the smuggled rubies. Zhang and his men ate quickly and left. So, I predict we'll hear from them sooner rather than later."

"Sooner, I hope," said Boc. "Great news."

"Well, I'm confident it will all be wrapped up before long," smiled Kimsan. "I'll investigate the financial sources further while our Triad friends deal with the smuggling matter. Then, when it's all over, the Team can return the favor for the *Chao pho* by informing the *Bangkok Scimitar* about how the local Mafias, attentive to their civic responsibilities, helped rid Bangkok of this despicable heart saga.

"Now, before you gentlemen go, there is a second point to consider. The Council of Elders wants to invite our Chinese friend, Zhang Min, to join our associated groups. He is a modern leader, highly sophisticated and exacting in the Chinese manner. He leads an important Triad and is relentlessly persuasive in an iron-fisted sense.

"Since the Chinese are important friends of Cambodia, our Council colleagues feel our association needs someone like Zhang Min. What is your thinking?"

"We vote yes, right, Boc?"

"Definitely."

"Then I'll keep you posted."

38. Demonstrating the System

It was a cloudless day when the DHC-3 Otter from Naypyidaw, Burma, set down at Don Muang Airport in Bangkok and taxied to the aviation business center. The pilot turned the aircraft over for fueling while arranging the return flight plan. Dr. Oo exited beneath the wing, white smile blazing, and entered the lounge where Drs. Hu, Julian, and Angela waited with the demo VR Surgery package. Dr. Oo bobbed on his toes as they exchanged wais.

Dr. Hu said, "It looks like a great day for flying. But, first, let me introduce Drs. Angela Tran and Julian Debois who always assist me. They know the Sino system inside and out."

"Hello, Doctors. I'm excited to have you for the demo."

"I'm delighted that you opted to try the system. I hope you'll enjoy the demo program today and use the full-up system regularly after it's delivered," said Hu. "Every week, users remark on how it's improved their surgical technique. We expect you will find the system helpful, too."

"I'm sure I will," said Dr. Oo. "We've scheduled a room for our training and practice sessions. My scrub nurse, Sanda, will help you set things up."

"Excellent, excellent," said Dr. Hu. "I'm excited to meet your team and look forward to a grand tour of the hospital."

"Of course," said Oo. "I think you will be impressed. Naypyidaw is Burma's new capital, and we're still building the city, but the pagoda and the hospital are completely finished. In fact, we are now the largest specialty hospital in Burma. Naypyidaw is located just a few hundred kilometers from Yangon and about three hundred from Mandalay. Our urgent patients come by helicopter from those cities and otherwise by car or ambulance.

"A terrific twenty-lane highway leads from the airport almost to our doorstep. A Tatmadaw Air Force general insisted on building a highway that could serve as an emergency landing strip. So he loans this plane to the hospital. Our administrator is proud of the hospital and will enjoy showing you around."

As the plane warmed up, Hu's team stowed the SinoAI system and climbed in behind the pilot and Dr. Oo while Julian took a rear seat. As they chatted, Dr. Oo boasted that the 150-bed hospital was built—rooms, halls, WCs, closets, ORs, everything—all in three weeks!

"You see, with the negative international reaction to Suu Kyi's house arrest, the junta scrambled to avoid further adverse publicity. So, they repurposed the prefab materials originally intended for building prison camps to construct our hospital instead. The general who loans us this plane helped make that happen.

"We might not even need an internment camp if our minorities would settle down," Oo commented casually. "The Rohingya are restless and starting to leave the country."

"I'd worry about the ghosts of imprisoned people who died unjustly in military detention," ventured Hu. "What if their spirits traveled with the prefab materials to your hospital?"

"Nonsense," said Oo leaning back over his shoulder. "Everybody in my village believed in ghosts, but I outgrew that stuff. I think ghosts are hokum promoted by shamans. Still, I'll admit to a bit of chill in my surgical suite at night. Maybe I should adjust the air conditioning.

"When we tour the hospital, you'll see that the rooms are quite comfortable. They hardly look like detainment cells. Most of them look out on the golden Uppatasanti pagoda—it's a copy of the famous Shwesandaw Pagoda in Yangon. The hospital received state support since we are in the capital city. I think we've made good use of their trust."

On the flight to Naypyitaw, they admired the varied landscape below, first that of northwest Thailand and then over the Andaman Sea and the mouth of the great Irrawaddy River.

"The Irrawaddy River is Kipling's *Road to Mandalay*," Dr. Oo remarked. "I've only read the poem in translation, but it suggests that Kipling left his heart in Burma."

The word "heart" momentarily stopped the conversation until Angela filled the awkward silence with, "you are right, Dr. Oo. Kipling did leave his true love, *a sweeter maiden in a greener land* on the Irrawaddy's banks, and wished he could return."

Julian rolled his eyes.

The flight followed the Irrawaddy river northwards and arrived at Naypyidaw and the International Airport. The group deplaned in the misty morning heat and unloaded their gear. A Toyota SUV awaited their arrival and raced the group down a twenty-lane highway to the Capital General Hospital.

The single-story hospital was slick-sided, consistent with its prefabricated materials. Its small windows were barred, carrying harrowing implications of languishing souls rather than of reassurance of joy and cure. The limbs of an ancient Banyan tree shaded much of the building's lawn. Its epiphytic roots reached into the soil of the Irrawaddy plain.

An attendant hurried to the SUV, waied all around, and retrieved the Virtual Reality system's cases while the administrator welcomed Hu's group into the hospital.

A pharmacy dispensary was on the immediate left, and a few patients occupied a large waiting room on the right. Reception lay straight ahead, managed by several women in hospital uniforms. Wide halls on either side led into the hospital's interior. Everything appeared professional, clean, and efficient.

Dr. Oo had organized a conference room near the surgical suites with racks for the VR equipment around a mock-up OR and surgical instrument tables. Before the surgical demo began, Dr. Hu invited Dr. Oo and Sanda to enjoy the immersive experience of a VR stroll through a teak forest. Hu fitted them with the mesh sensor caps that would dissolve the barrier between their inner worlds and the computer inputs.

"So here's a short travelogue to help you get accustomed to the virtual environment."

Dr. Oo and Sanda ooh'd and aah'd as they wandered along the virtual jungle trail. They heard birds squawk and monkeys chit-chit and, in the distance, a running stream. Sanda raised her foot to step over a root on the trail. They pointed out things to each other. "That one's been collared and is drying out," said Oo, pointing to a teak tree whose outer layers were cut through circumferentially. "Collaring dries them out enough to float downriver." Oo lurched, apparently dodging a length of hanging vine.

"Are you okay?" Hu asked.

Oo said, "This is amazing. I'm sorry we have to stop."

After the forest demo, they prepared for the surgical event. "How will I hand the instruments to Dr. Oo?" was Sanda's first question. "Do I just pass them the way I usually do, or what?"

"Use them the way you usually do. The program will alert you if there is a better way. Same for Dr. Oo. It's impossible to explain how the system works, but empirically the virtual world becomes the real world. In this world, instrument handling and operating actually train your surgical skills, muscle memory, and procedural understanding.

"So, our instruments relate to each other according to an AI-swarm algorithm. They know where they are in space, and proprioceptive—haptic—feedback sets a user's manual expectations."

"Whoa, too much information, thank you, Dr. Hu," said Dr. Oo. "Let's get on within the surgery."

Sanda and Oo lowered their heads as Hu fitted their neuro sensor caps again in preparation for this first experience.

"Good. We'll start the demonstration scenario," said Hu. "You and Sanda will be in a virtual OR completely indistinguishable from your real one, including the personnel, sights, and typical sounds. The anesthesiologist will have your 'patient' asleep, and the pump tech will operate the bypass equipment as usual. Finally, the patient—a perfect 3-D computer-generated human—will be prepped for the midline sternal incision. You can use the foot pedal to move back and forth through your operation or ask the invisible surgeon advisor for suggestions.

"So, now you need to make a choice. On the one hand, you can first observe the virtual surgeon doing the case or proceed directly to operate by yourself. What's your preference? I'll select it for you this time."

"Let's skip the demo surgeon. I'll start fresh," said Dr. Oo.

"OK. Remember, the system will beep to let you know if you're doing something incorrectly or that surgeons have never done before. If so, you can use the foot pedal to go back a few seconds and try again or ask the virtual surgeon to demo the move," Dr. Hu instructed. "So, use the foot pedal to go back and forth. To end the session, press the foot pedal quickly three times.

"Sanda will pass the instruments correctly. Starting the countdown: Ten, nine, eight, ...one! GO!"

"Knife, please, Sanda." Sanda snapped Oo's knife into his hand and offered fingertip pressure on skin edges for light retraction as Dr. O made the midline incision. The look and feel of the flesh and the cutting sensation were real to him. He applied clips to stop the skin edge bleeding and placed retractors to hold the tissues back. The suction hissed. Oo requested a periosteal elevator and felt resistance as he lifted the fascia. The electrocautery buzzed when he coagulated bleeders. Sanda passed the bone saw to Oo, and he cut the sternum. The saw vibrated in his hand, and Sanda suctioned away the cloud of bone dust. She passed him the sternal retractor. He inserted its blades and cranked the chest open. And there it was, the virtual heart beating within the pericardium, the EKG monitor beeping in concert. Oo incised the pericardium and watched the heart bounce with every pulse. His breath caught at the reality. The anesthesiologist injected 35,000u of Heparin to thin the blood. Next, the anesthesiologist infused the cardioplegic drug to reversibly stop the heart. Dr.Oo would place the patient on the heart-lung machine, the 'pump". The pump would keep the patient alive by pulsing freshly oxygenated blood into the patient's vascular system and allowing Dr. Oo to operate in a bloodless field.

First, however, Dr. Oo summoned the virtual surgeon to demonstrate the complex technical choreography of going 'on pump'. The virtual expert placed a cannula into the right atrium to collect venous blood returning to the heart and direct this blue blood into the oxygenator. He then inserted an arterial cannula into the aorta, which delivered fresh red blood from the pump. It was so real! So much so that everyone took a deep breath when the perfusionist said, "on-pump." The pump had restored the patient's systemic circulation. In the operating room, everyone's heart beat faster, except for the patient's. It was motionless and ready to be fixed.

Releasing the virtual surgeon, Dr. Oo prepared to repeat the steps that the expert had just performed. "Okay, I'm ready to do it myself," Oo said. Everyone held their breath as he began.

Right away, Oo fumbled the right atrial cannulation. He tried again and fumbled again, then tried a bicalval cannulation unsuccessfully. "Why not try it this way," the program pleasantly prompted. Oo tried again but failed and was prompted again. The continuing prompts so annoyed Dr. Oo that he stomped on the foot pedal, slammed his instruments down, and aborted the procedure. Embarrassed, he tried to laugh off his tantrum, saying, "I'm glad SinoAI plans to ship my order soon. I'll benefit from the system."

"Of course," said Dr. Hu. "This was your first time out. It's complex. You'll get used to it with practice."

"Why don't we tour the hospital?" suggested the administrator, who had been standing at the OR door.

The hospital was well maintained, polished and immaculate. Orderlies in pressed whites escorted patients around, and speakers paged hospital personnel as is universally typical. The rooms looked modern, spacious, and furnished with familiar hospital appointments. A small window from each room opened into the hall. "Designed to pass food and samples back and forth easily," explained the administrator. Unfortunately, the doors appeared to lock from the hall side only. Glancing through the room, Angela and Julian noted bars on the outside of the windows. This design was definitely in keeping with the dual-use prefabricated units.

As they passed down the next hall, a feeble voice cried out in a melodic accent. They saw a dark-skinned young patient whose face and eyes had an Indian look about them. Gesticulating pleadingly, he appealed in English for help. His intent was clear, but his strength was waning, his language growing indecipherable.

"Don't worry. We are on the psych ward now," said Dr. Oo. "That man is a Rohingya. None of them live in Naypyidaw. This one was hauled in from the Buddhist-Muslim riots. There's been an uptick in ethnic violence. And now, a so-called revolt of Buddhist monks is brewing."

"Yeah, our papers say that the junta keeps hundreds of minority dissidents in the Insein Prison under inhumane conditions, though the military denies repression of minorities. Many ethnic people have fled to Thailand," said Julian.

"Typical anti-junta propaganda, I'd say," said Oo. "You can tell by looking that man isn't native Burmese. Has a Rohingya look about him. They claim their RaKyine State was here several thousand years ago, but the history is cloudy; so, who knows?" said Dr. Oo carelessly. "Real

Burmese don't like them. I suppose the feeling is mutual because so many Rohingyas are heading for Bangladesh. Of course, they are lying to the world about persecution. But don't get me started. I say 'live and let live,'" Oo continued, smiling.

A look of nausea passed Julian's face at this sanctimonious 'live-and-let-live' pronouncement.

The administrator, sensing unease, suggested they have a bite in the hospital cafeteria before flying back to Bangkok. They passed a hall with an arrow and sign that read, 'Crematorium'.

"It may seem unusual to have a crematorium connected with a hospital," said the administrator. "Sends the wrong message, perhaps—but people always enjoy a ceremony in the shadow of the grand Uppatasanti Pagoda. The pagoda contains the tooth relic of the Buddha from China and four jadeite green Buddha images," said the administrator importantly. "Also, a general gifted the bones of the Buddha's forefinger."

The pagoda's magnificent golden dome floated above the hospital, the diamond bud at its apex occasionally glinting when the clouds parted. It was said to be visible from every road leading into Naypyidaw.

They enjoyed classic Mohinga, the national dish of soup and noodles, and green tea for lunch. Afterward, they wandered toward the hospital exit making small talk. The SUV now cooled beneath the ficus tree. An orderly had loaded the demo equipment. The administrator waved them goodbye, and Dr. Oo accompanied them to the airport, where he said goodbye at the DHC-3 Otter's door. Dr. Hu promised he would personally deliver Oo's VR system as soon as it arrived.

Once inside the plane, only the prop stir was heard. Julian asked Angela, "So, what would your Rudyard Kipling think about our day, Angela?"

"After today, I doubt he'd leave his heart in Burma."

"For fear of what might happen to it, you mean?"

"Of course."

39. Inside Dr. Oo

"OK, Milo, Wisut, it's time to employ the bot strategy," Angela confirmed when they returned from Naypyidaw. "Dr. Oo's the surgeon we're looking for. We've seen him in his native habitat, and it's not pretty. He's the one. Hu, Julian, and I agree."

"Whoa, you mean this fidgety, engaging surgeon, who bears the weight of Burma's cardiac ill on his shoulders; this man who purchases the VR system on the spot; this same man is the villain?"

"Okay, okay. When Dr. Oo strode up to the exhibit booth, your sarcasm apart, he seemed benignly eccentric. That was on first impression," Hu admitted. "But that evening, I reflected on the day's events. A sixth sense alerted me that something didn't fit. I began to wonder about the guy, to have doubts. Yes, even then.

"So, we were determined to get a reading on Dr. Oo's inner self, to observe his behavior, coax his nature out in conversation, learn who this man is inside, before unleashing digital tricks. And did we ever!"

"Yeah," Julian said, "Dr. Oo's charm wore off quickly. He blew up at surgery and dismissed the virtual surgeon after screwing up repeatedly. Finally, Oo stomped on the foot pedal hard enough to break it. I was afraid he'd start throwing the instruments. After that, he acted embarrassed and tried to laugh his tantrum off, saying he needed practice."

"He does, in fact," said Hu. "He's obviously incompetent."

"Yet he calls himself a cardiac surgeon?" Wisut remarked.

"Yes, either he lacks personal insight or considers himself above it all as Burma's only cardiac surgeon. Or simply doesn't care," said Angela.

"For me, his indifference to the plight of minorities and his contempt for the suffering Rohingya patient on the psych ward was sickening," Julian added, "I'm reading an arrogant man who is dismissive of authority, impatient, and indifferent to people. I may not be a psychiatrist, but he's a psychopath to my mind."

"So, Wisut, will your bots understand that this man's white-tooth ebullience and charm disguise a black heart?" asked Angela.

"Don't worry about it," said Wisut in his best New York accent. "It's under control. Malcolm has made sure the Bots' interactions with Oo will be credible, while Tanaka has ensured their appropriate physical expressions—smiles, gestures, etc. Your job is to develop scenarios that Dr. Oo will find medically credible and decide when the bots should appear during surgery. And, not least, who they personify."

"Who they will be is the easiest," said Hu. "I vote for Julian's suggestion to use two patients who died at the hands of Dr. Oo, the Rohingya we saw in the hospital and the British gentleman. They should show up just when the surgery seems to be going perfectly. Surprise, Dr. Oo, guess who!"

"Brilliant," Julian and Angela agreed.

40. Mr. Woods

"Hold on, please," Milo smiled, and passed the phone to Kiet. "It's for Khun Prasert; Khun Sathit is calling from the Royal Facets Complex."

"Khun Sathit, what a pleasure! How are you today?" Kiet asked.

"Never better, thanks. A guest, Mr. Woods, who fits your description, has just checked in with two attendants."

"Hoo-ah! Are his attendants still there?"

"Yes," said Sathit, "a nurse and an attendant, whom I call Khun Pompadour; you'll see why."

"I'm on my way. Bye now," said Kiet. Then, turning to Milo, "Another probable transplant patient has arrived at the RFC Hotel."

Within the hour, a well-dressed gentleman with shined leather shoes stepped into the lobby of the RFC hotel. His name tag identified him as a hotel consultant. "Good morning, Khun Sathit," Kiet said.

"My goodness, Khun Prasert," said Sathit, catching her breath. "Uh, so, how do you want to handle this?"

"First, Sathit, my name is really Kiet. 'Prasert' is my name as a hotel consultant. Can't pretend I like it. So, my name is Kiet, okay?"

"*That* Kiet, the Muay Thai champion?"

"More accurately, a former contender. I never made it to the final round. So, are they still in the room? Where is Mr. Woods from?"

"Yes, they are in the room, and Mr. Woods is from the US. His nurse speaks marginal Thai and some English, but Khun Pompadour speaks mainly Burmese. Looks like a muscle man stuffed into snappy clothes."

"Thanks, I imagine we'll have a friendly encounter, but you may want to step back if it gets testy," said Kiet.

"Don't worry about me. But Kiet, you wouldn't want to wrinkle those fine clothes if physical persuasion is required," Sathit said flirtatiously.

"Oh, these clothes," Kiet blushed, his face darkening. "They are lightweight with plenty of spandex."

"Stretchy and ready for action, I'll bet," Sathit continued to flirt. "I've practiced martial arts myself and know about stretchy clothing."

"I see," said Kiet. "I feel safer knowing about your martial arts. Hope we don't need them."

Kiet and Sathit arrived at the guest's heavy, key-carded door and knocked. After the peephole darkened, the nurse cracked the door open, "Yes, can I help you?" Kiet inserted his foot and pushed open the door wider. "Yes, you can. We are here to see Khun Woods."

A large man with a mound of slicked-backed hair emerged from a bedroom looking unfriendly. The nurse drew back toward the kitchenette. A wheelchair stood near a closed door.

"Mr. Woods is not receiving visitors," Khun Pompadour growled. "And who are you to burst in like this? Show me some ID, or I'll call security."

Kiet ignored the bluster. "We want to speak with Mr. Woods. Get him out here now." Sathit eyed the nurse.

"You are looking for trouble," Khun Pompadour said. He moved toward Kiet and was suddenly on the floor, unconscious but breathing. Kiet brushed his trouser leg. "It's spandex," Kiet said and winked at Sathit, who was disarming the nurse who had raised a butcher knife.

"Drop it, or your wrist is mine." The knife fell to the floor.

"Awesome martial arts, Sathit," Kiet said, admiring how she immobilized the nurse.

Flipping open his phone, Kiet called Saw, "Bring the TopazEV around and notify the hospital guard that a delivery is coming his way." Then he called Angela.

"I'm on the way," she said.

When Angela arrived, Kiet and Sathit had already flex-cuffed the befuddled Khun Pompadour, hefted him into the car, and covered him with a blanket. Kiet had flex-cuffed the nurse, too. Sathit handed Kiet their phones and took the wheelchair.

"I'll check on Mr. Woods first and meet you at the hospital," Angela said.

"What a day!" Kiet said to Sathit just before leaving. "Maybe we can do something tonight; talk, go to the gym, and have dinner afterward at *Tii Baan*?"

Sathit smiled, "Just tell me the time."

41. The Nurse and Khun Pompadour

The TopazEV conveyed Kiet and the two attendants to the loading dock of the Ratchathewi hospital. Angela whispered up on her motorcycle shortly after. The security guard recognized the elegantly dressed Kiet as the Kiet of black leather, who had sworn him to silence. He whispered to Kiet that he had held his tongue.

"Thanks, Pal," Kiet said to the guard and slipped him a few hundred Baht. "Let's find a wheelchair for the wobbly man there."

The guard got a wheelchair and, with Kiet's help, hauled the groggy Khun Pompadour from the car. The tone of Kiet's voice encouraged the nurse to come along too.

"There are people inside," the guard said. "Sorry, I don't have a phone and couldn't alert you."

Nurses and orderlies moved about the hospital, presumably preparing for a new patient. Kiet informed them their patient was not coming and asked if they expected anyone else to arrive.

"They answered probably not. Nonetheless, Kiet wanted to move along quickly and commanded, "Saw, roll the husky gentleman into the cold room and the lady with him. Unzip the body bag, let it breathe, and let them reflect on their situation."

Affecting politeness, Saw escorted Khun Pompadour and the nurse into the cold room, hurried out, and closed the door with a familiar wumph. "Phew," he said. "Can't say the cold has preserved the poor gentleman. He looks like he's about to pop. I hate to think of zipping the bag up again."

"Yes, looks like our detainees have noticed too," said Kiet. They were furiously pounding on the door, overlooking the safety latch inside. "Let us out," they bawled.

Kiet nodded affirmatively, and Saw opened the door. The nurse and Khun Pompadour propelled themselves out ahead of the billowing cloud of mist, flex-cuffed hands across their mouths, gagging. After they settled down, the nurse recognized Saw, "But, but. You are..."

"Yes, he's the driver," interrupted Kiet. "He values his life and is helping us out, and I expect you to do the same. You probably saw the stack of empty body bags, right? The operative word being empty. We want them to stay that way."

"We saw the bags by that poor dead man. He's not our doing. We just take orders from a boss who sends us to pick up patients. We've never seen the guy," she said. "He notifies us when a patient is ready for pickup and puts us in charge. We pay the referring doctor in cash and then fly back to Bangkok. The boss uses the RFC's 'luxury travel service' to bring patients through customs. We meet at the RFC Hotel and stay with patients until it's time for surgery, and Khun Saw comes for them. Then we are off duty until they call again when we reverse the process and accompany them back to their home country."

"How many have you accompanied back?" asked Angela.

"None, so far," answered the nurse. "Perhaps their recovery is slow, or they need prolonged physical therapy or something."

"Or something?" prompted Angela. "Nevermind. You know that you are in deep shit. The only way out is by cooperating with us.

"Let's begin with some names and demographics. Is this an international operation or restricted to California? Give us the Mr. Woods' California doctor's name, address, email, phone—everything you have. The same goes for other patients you've transported. How do crooked doctors get patients to take the bait? What's their usual cut? Are patients ambulatory or brought from a hospital? Who accepts the returning post-op patients—if any?"

"The California doctor is G. Gordon West, M.D.," the nurse replied. "We pick up patients from his office near the UC San Francisco hospital but not from the hospital. He medicates them before the trip, attests that they are stable, and sends their medicine along. Patients have never experienced cardiac complications on our trips. He bragged that he gets five thousand dollars per patient.

"We've brought six patients to Bangkok so far. Saw picked them up from the RFC Hotel for surgery. Our job is finished when a patient is ready to go home. The RFC hotel doesn't know what we are up to."

"You work for dangerous people and are quite expendable. They probably suspect you have screwed up and are already looking for you," Milo advised. "So, tell us what we need to know. Then I'll pass you to Colonel Amnat, our police chief. He's a fair man and will probably hold you in protective custody for now. You are accessories to horrific crimes, and I advise you to come clean with the colonel. Your cooperation may depend on whether you go to trial or be released with new identities."

"We'll get Mr. Woods back to California."

The two remained flex-cuffed until the colonel's men picked them up. Milo was pleased to inform the team's UN contact of the good day's work.

42. Nice to Have Your Own Gym

This had been a terrifically successful day for the team, not to mention a lifesaving one for Mr. Woods. The events had also ignited the smoldering attraction between Kiet and Sathit. As planned earlier, they met for dinner at *Tii Baan*.

When Sathit stepped into the restaurant, Milo did a double-take but quickly recovered and welcomed her with a wai. Sathit's hair was midnight-blue, worn swept above the ears and drawn back. Her jeans fit exquisitely, and her burgundy tank, cut at the midriff, emphasized her six-pack and 'innie' navel. She had brought along her gym bag. Kiet stood from a nearby table, caught his breath, and greeted her.

"How did things end up with Mr. Woods?" Sathit asked. "Is he safe?"

"Angela and Saw delivered him to the airport," Kiet said. "Mr. Woods thought his surgery plans were on the up and up but was thrilled to head home alive after learning otherwise."

Changing the subject, Kiet remarked, "You should have seen the awesome move Sathit made on the nurse, Milo," Kiet remarked. "She wasn't kidding about martial arts training."

"I can believe it," Milo observed.

"Well, I practice," said Sathit. "But I never saw anyone hit the floor as fast as Khun Pompadour after whatever Kiet did."

Milo mumbled something, gestured to a convenient table, excused himself, and ducked behind the bar. Kiet and Sathit enjoyed a light dinner under the ceiling fans. As the regulars trickled in, *Hotel California* played in the background. Fortunately, Milo hadn't begun to sing.

After a light dinner, Kiet suggested they stroll by Peace Park and come back for a workout. "I want you to see my gym," Kiet added.

"Kiet, I have a question," Sathit said as they strolled past the park fountain. "You retired just as the Muay Thai championships were starting, didn't you?"

"I hated to do it, but my opponent dealt me a knee in the ribs that brought me down as fast as Khun Pompadour today. Broken ribs and a punctured lung ended my fighting days. But I had fought twenty bouts at Lumpini stadium. Not so bad."

"I'll bet there's still fight left in you. Maybe you can show me some tricks when we get back. I brought my gym bag," Sathit smiled.

Kiet had finished blushing by the time they returned from their jog in the park. "Well, here it is," Kiet said. "Not bad for a personal gym, huh?"

"Wow, it's the real thing; there's even a climbing rope," Sathit noted. "Do you think I can shinny up a rope?" she winked at Kiet.

They stepped behind screens to change into gym clothes.

By the time Kiet had his gym shoes on, Sathit was halfway up the thick rope, entwining it between her feet and squeezing the rope between her thighs in rhythm with her hand-over-hand pulls. The rope created intimate sensations as it glided between her thighs, up her abdomen, and between her breasts as she moved upwards. Arriving at the top, Satit winked at Kiet and slid slowly down, smiling.

A patina of sweat covered Sathit's skin, and her muscles stood out. As her toes came to the floor. Kiet moved behind to stabilize her dismount. Then, releasing the rope, she relaxed back onto him. His arms encircled her, and his nails glided up her abdomen and approached her sports bra. As his hands brushed her breasts, Sathit reached behind her. "Ooo," she said, catching her breath, "Bamboo!" They were quickly entangled on the mat, and the day's excitement climaxed in a crescendo.

They dressed slowly and, nuzzling, returned to *Tii Baan* for a nightcap. Chua smiled as she took their drink orders.

43. Yee Revealed

"Saw, stop polishing the damn car and get in here," demanded a voice from within the embassy. Security pointed Saw up the stairs to the second floor. "Where the hell is that new patient, Mr. Woods, and where are his attendants, the nurse, and that slick-haired muscle man? The RFC desk says they left. What's happened to them? Where did you take them?"

"Nowhere, Boss. I didn't take them anywhere. I heard they came in last night. I went by the RFC hotel this morning, and they were gone."

"What the hell! Something is wrong! So, you went by the hotel, parked the car, got out, hauled your miserable ass to reception, and inquired politely for them, did you?" the boss said.

"Yes, I did. The reception desk told me the Woods party left without checking out. Apparently, guests come and go, tour the city or simply take a walk. So, nothing seemed unusual. They checked Mr. Wood's record, and his passport was gone. She suggested they might have gone to the bank," Saw responded.

"Bank my ass. They didn't go to any damned bank! Something's up," the boss lifted a red-colored phone to call his counterpart in Burma. He barked into the receiver, "It's me."

From the other end of the line, Saw heard a crackling voice, "Well, no shit. What do you want?" Saw noted the boss's name on an ostentatious brass plate on his desk, Na Yee. Saw could remember that name.

"Something is not right," Yee said. "Our patient and his attendants have disappeared. They got to the hotel but left."

The voice on the other end asked, "Have you been by the surgery hospital yet?"

"Uh, no, not yet."

"Then get your fat ass over there and check it out. Maybe they went there," the other party shouted. "We've got huge money in this. If you've fucked things up, you'd better not plan to come home." Saw pretended not to hear the conversation or the other party slam the receiver down.

"What now, Khun Yee?" Saw asked.

"Have security bring the car up and open the gate! We're going to the hospital."

Saw had turned his iPhone to Record and hoped it had captured something from Yee's call, especially the command to go to the hospital. Then, when Saw called gate security, he also texted the recording to Milo, Angela, and Kiet, hoping there was time for somebody to do something.

The usual protesters had assembled outside the Embassy of the Republic of the Union of Myanmar, causing Saw to creep out when the gate opened and thread the car through the crowd. Protesters pounded the rooftop, slapped the windows, and shouted their demands. "Get on through these idiots, Saw, and be quick about it," Yee growled as protesters waved signs demanding, 'Save the Rohingya', 'Shwe to the Criminal Court', 'Free the Lady!'. He sneered at them and shook his fists.

A creature of the desk and swivel chair, Yee had no feel for Bangkok's layout or a route to the Ratchathewi hospital; so Saw took a long way around. He hit every stoplight. As they finally pulled up, the security guard recognized Saw's car. He opened the boss's door, led the way to the back entrance, swept open the heavy door, theatrically gestured Yee in, and abruptly slammed the door shut behind him. Saw's recording had gotten through.

The guard smiled and said, "Don't worry about it. Kiet and Angela are already here, and Milo is com...well, here he is now!"

Milo strode up.

44. Poor Khun Yee

Yee stumbled almost into Angela's hands. "Khun Yee, how nice of you to join us. I am Doctor Tran," she said, wrestling Yee into a wheelchair. "We were hoping our chief would already be here, but ...oh, here he is now. Welcome to the gathering, Milo. Let me introduce our guest, Khun Yee," said Angela, affecting a polite formality. "Khun Na Yee is from the Burmese embassy. I doubt he usually looks so rumpled, but he struggled as we assisted him into the wheelchair. He speaks functional Thai, atonally, perhaps, but okay."

"My pleasure, Khun Yee," said Milo, offering an ironic wai to Yee, whose arms were bound to the wheelchair arms.

"Who the hell are you?' Yee sneered. "I have diplomatic immunity. If you know what's good for you, you will immediately let me out of here."

"Didn't I say you checked your diplomatic immunity at the door?" interrupted Angela. "You mustn't confuse diplomatic immunity with the impunity of the life without consequences your family leads in Burma."

She continued, "Is your daddy the infamous General Yee? So are you a chip off the old block, Yee? I hear blood runs thick in the general's family, as thick as blood in the streets of Rangoon after a good massacre. Or are you an unappreciated bastard son? Did your daddy ship you to Bangkok to get you out of his sight?"

"I don't know what you are getting at, you arrogant bitch," Yee snarled, avoiding Angela's eyes. "I have diplomatic immunity, and you'd better get me out of here! You and these jerks will pay for this big time!"

"Of course," said Milo. "I'm sure you don't enjoy being lectured by a woman doctor. So, why don't we wheel you around for hospital rounds, see some patient rooms and the surgical suites, cool off a bit, and perhaps meet a patient."

"What are you up to?" growled Yee, his face growing darker by the minute.

"Well, Yee, we are 'up to' getting some answers from you. So we are going to give you a quiz during rounds. Simple questions, nothing complicated," said Milo in a benign tone. "Something about heart transplant tourism and your organization."

"Fuck you and fuck your quiz. Get me my phone," Yee demanded.

"Well, then, let's skip the quiz for now and begin the tour."

Angela led them along the gleaming hall, pointing at various things: here a patient room, there the operating room, and, "Oh my, a heart-lung machine! What about that, Khun Yee, my goodness, a heart pump oxygenator?" said Angela. The tour ended at the stainless door of the cold storage room. "While you are here, Khun Yee, perhaps you would also like to meet a patient."

Kiet opened the door and wheeled Yee into the cold miasma. A single bulb dimly outlined the body bag. Kiet shut the door with the usual hermetic whoomph. "This will help Khun Yee cool off, huh guys?"

After a moment, Yee screamed, then retched. They could hear Yee's muffled cries. Angela was afraid he might aspirate vomitus during his herky-jerky breathing and would die before he had time for the quiz.

"I know a little panic can facilitate an interrogation, Milo. But we can't examine a dead man," said Angela. "Let's get him out now."

Kiet opened the door and shoved Yee's wheelchair into the hall. Disoriented and, blinded by tears, Yee almost tipped the chair over.

"Look at you," said Milo. "You have vomited on yourself, and, look, you've lost control of your bladder. You smell terrible. Let's let the man stand up and get those clothes changed." Yee stripped and covered himself modestly with his hands. They hosed Yee down and tossed him a scrub suit. He began to shiver uncontrollably and begged, "I've got a bad heart. Lay off."

"You've got a bad heart?" spat Angela. "How about the guy in the bag, you shrivelled-dick bastard. He came 3500 kilometers to get a new heart. Instead, he's in a body bag. His chest is wide open. There's a heart in it, alright. But it's not the one he came with. His new one probably belonged to a young Rohingya whose heart your gang stole and whose body they threw away."

"I don't know anything about that guy in the bag or any dead Rohingya or any damned stolen heart," Yee protested.

Angela continued her scold, "You are a heartless piece of shit, Yee. Your young 'donor' is heartless, too, literally. For all we know, his corpse lies in some forsaken rice paddy or feeds fish in the Irrawaddy. Or, maybe, he came out of the hospital crematorium below the Uppatasanti Pagoda as dust in an urn. I'd guess he had the look of India about him before he 'donated', not the light, smooth skin of a real Burmese. He was maybe in his twenties, healthy, probably a family man, a husband, and a father. But he disappeared one day. You bastards actually do this shit," she fumed.

"I don't know what you are talking about," muttered Yee through chattering Teeth.

"Okay, let's all relax," said Milo. "Yee here will tell us everything we need to know unless he needs more time for thought." Let's stop scolding him and ask nicely

"Don't put me back in there. I told you I've got heart trouble. I'd die," said Yee.

"Worse things could happen," said Milo introspectively. "For balance, you would depart this world as you came in: Naked and screaming."

"Should I help him in right now?" Kiet asked, looking toward the stainless door.

"Hold off for a moment, Kiet," Milo said. "Let's not wheel this poor man in again yet. Remember his bad heart. We need to pass him alive to the Bangkok police. They will hold him for the UN authorities, who worry about human rights violations, perhaps ethnic cleansing in Burma. I believe genocide is another word they use. How about that, Yee? Bad outlook."

"Okay, okay, but no more cold room," Yee whined.

"We won't let you die today, Khun Yee," Milo said. "Flex cuff him. I'll call Colonel Amnat, our police chief. I assisted him last year with the international technicalities of rescuing a kidnapped Thai child, so he gave me his private number. Then I'll call our UN liaison."

Milo got the Colonel on the phone. "No, Amnat, there's not a bruise on him," said Milo. "He is shivering in a scrub suit and appears scared shitless.

"Yes, we have proof that he's involved with the illicit trade in human hearts and probably with ethnic cleansing and crimes against humanity. His colleagues will want to avoid a trip to The Hague and may try to silence him. Our UN agent will call you within the hour and probably have an Interpol officer here by sunset.

"Yes; no worries, Pal, just doing my job," said Milo. "We are at the Ratchatewi Hospital. Come in through the loading dock. Yee's trussed up in a wheelchair. The security guard will be expecting you. We'll see you when you get here.

"Just a heads up, Colonel, a former transplant patient is in the cold room. He's been there for a while, so moving him will be an undesirable task. And for the public record, we aren't involved. I suggest you get some photos. The *Bangkok Scimitar* will praise you for finally solving this international case."

Later that evening, Team Bangkok met in *Tii Baan*, their mood triumphant but unsettled—they might still be in danger. Angela summed up the situation with a Texas metaphor, "So we've cut off the rattle, but the fangs can still strike us. We've got to stay alert."

"Thank you for that picturesque analysis," Kiet said, smiling.

Toward the end of the meeting, much of the team had filtered away. Boc and Khem were having a smoke and invited Milo to join them for a beer. They tapped bottlenecks and toasted.

After a few swigs, Khem said, "Kimsan says that things are looking good, that he's focused on Burma, and Zhang Min's group is seriously pissed off."

"Thanks for telling me," said Milo. "Kimsan seems like a man of action. I wish I knew him better."

"I have a feeling you will," said Khem.

"That's for sure," Boc added.

45. Big Day of Tricks

Several days after Yee's apprehension, the three doctors boarded the Otter for the hour's flight to Naypyidaw International Airport. They brought the full-up SinoAI participatory VR equipment and arranged it in the Otter's storage area. Dr. Hu wore his most innocent face as he chatted with the pilot. "Yes, Bangkok's Don Muang was becoming my favorite airport," the pilot said, making idle conversation.

"Oh, yeah? You fly into Bangkok often?" Hu said, making casual conversation.

"More and more, about once a week for the last couple of months, carrying Dr. Oo and his cooler of medications—for eye patients or diabetics—whichever. I love the Bangkok runs, but Dr. Oo will take over soon enough. He is working on his instrument rating. Other parties also lease this plane from the General. So maybe they will hire me."

Hu's benign expression almost shattered. This new information added to the tension surrounding the imminent deployment of the deep fake.

"This plane is a workhorse, the classic bush plane," the pilot went on without pause. It'll carry anything you can get through the door, and the storage area is infinitely reconfigurable. Often enough, other passengers fly to Bangkok with the general, carrying considerable baggage; no idea who they are, but they sound like people from the Shan region near China and Laos."

"How interesting. Other doctors, or...?"

"No, I'd say more likely businessmen."

When the Otter touched down, an assistant gathered the VR equipment and apologized for Dr. Oo, who was tied up in surgery, and the administrator, who was out raising money for a new children's wing. "Yeah, right," Hu muttered.

The Uppatasanti Pagoda rose golden in the distance as they headed along the wide highway into the city. Angela announced that the pagoda looked like a golden Hershey's kiss with a few spiky stupas standing alongside.

"My, aren't we irreverent today!" sniffed Julian.

"Just trying to lighten the atmosphere," Angela said.

When they drove up, Dr. Oo bounded from the hospital and welcomed them with an exuberant wai and blazing smile, "Sawatdii-krap, Sawatdii-krap. The room is ready for the VR system; instruments, cameras, computers, and whatever else. I can't wait to scrub in," Dr. Oo said, bouncing on tiptoes.

"Glad to see you so enthusiastic," said Dr. Hu. "I'm certain the system will meet your expectations." Julian and Angela helped Sanda set it up, and Dr. Oo put on the mesh cap, preparing himself for their procedure.

"First of all, Dr. Oo, I'm sure you remember that our system presents an interactive virtual world where your surgery is totally realistic. You can select any procedure from the list of surgeries performed by real-world surgical masters and do it yourself," Hu began.

"You'll work with Sanda using your own instruments. You'll see and interact with a virtual anesthesiologist and pump tech performing their supporting jobs, observe the monitors on the walls, hear normal OR sounds, and the like. You don't just watch surgery; you perform it. Thus the concept of participatory augmented VR.

"Again, I advise first-time users to access and watch the virtual expert surgeon before performing a procedure themselves. The experts always make difficult surgery look easy, and you can learn their tricks. After that, practice, practice, practice until the procedure is your own."

"I know, I know! You said this during your demo!"

"Nonetheless, it's helpful to rehearse. Select a given procedure—a valve replacement today, isn't it?—and participate with an expert first. Afterward, you can go back in and do the same case yourself as the primary surgeon as often as you like."

Dr. Oo shifted from foot to foot and fiddled with his surgical mask as Hu continued to talk.

"Okay, Dr. Oo, I know. We've already covered this, but it bears repeating.

"Remember, in addition to the procedures done by experts, we also have built-in example techniques distilled from hundreds of videos. So, every technique the world's best surgeons have used and their mistakes are at your fingertips. In addition, the system will alert you to better techniques and possible errors, allowing you to learn best practices virtually before operating on living patients.

"As you personally experienced, the alerts and prompts can be more annoying than illuminating, despite their obvious value. But, do try to put up with any frustrations the prompts may cause. You'll soon get comfortable with such oversight."

"I get it already!" sighed Oo. "I have done quite a lot of cardiac surgery myself. I'm Burma's only cardiac surgeon, you know. I just need some more tips and experience to stay current."

"Yes, Dr. Oo, but hang in with me. I have one last warning. This is very important! Interactions in our virtual environment are so real that several users have experienced temporary disorientation after finishing an operation and the mesh-array cap is off. In fact, some doctors have experienced true hallucinogenic states, thankfully temporary. But, some have lasted for hours to days."

"I'm not worried about that—no altered states for me. I was superstitious as a kid, but I'm agnostic to that stuff now," said Dr. Oo.

"Nonetheless, I am obliged to warn you," said Hu.

"I get it. Thank you for bringing the system and getting it up and running," said Dr. Oo. "I'll text for support if there's a problem. I want to get started right away."

"Yes, well, SinoAI is happy to be of service. We'll head back to Bangkok. Good luck, and do call if you need support. We are always there for you."

Dr. Oo thanked them, whisked them to the front door, and then turned and hurried back towards the VR room with an over-the-shoulder, "Safe travels!"

As the SUV sped down the highway, Hu whispered to Angela and Julian, "In case I haven't thanked you enough, I'm much obliged to you both for helping me through that awful Jaingshi period – without bots or a digital exorcism."

46. Cometh the Bots

The DHC-3 Otter lifted Drs Hu, Julian, and Angela into a cloudless sky above the green fields nourished by the muddy Irrawaddy. They appeared drowsy, almost drifting off, as the plane touched down at Don Muang in Bangkok. They headed back to the lab; there was nothing to do now but wait.

Back in Naypyidaw, Dr. Oo's scrub nurse, Sanda, had prepared everything for the procedure. The position sensors were attached to the instruments and the tracking cameras focused on the operating field. Blue tooth connected the system. Dr. Oo and Sanda adjusted their mesh-array caps and nodded at each other. It was finally time for some real virtual surgery."

"Turn us on, please, Sanda, and cue up the expert surgeon. I will be patient today and watch him do the case."

After concentrating on the expert's surgical technique, Oo hurried into the same valve replacement procedure, making the occasional mistake but proceeding carefully when prompted.

"Mistakes make the master," the expert voice reminded him. "You are doing fine."

"This couldn't be more real, could it, Sanda?" Oo asked.

"Almost beyond belief," she answered. "Amazing."

Oo seemed to fly through the case. Finishing, he removed the cannulas, patched the atrium and aorta, and said, "NOW!" The tech switched off the pump, and the anesthesiologist reversed the cardioplegic drug. The heart automatically resumed beating in normal sinus rhythm, and the mechanical valve clicked with each heartbeat. The thrill of success grew as tension surrendered its hold on the OR. Proud and delighted by his excellent result, Dr. Oo crowed, "Perfect; this is wonderful. Let's close him up, Sanda."

"Great job, Dr. Oo," Sanda said. Then, "Yuck, what is that weird squishing sound?"

Dr. Oo noticed it too. "It sounds like someone sloshing through mud or something."

"Or perhaps someone shuffling along in his own putrefaction Dr. Oo. Putrefaction is the word you're looking for, as in decay," a voice clarified. The fake was on. The first zombie-bot had emerged.

"What the—?" Oo glanced across the room. The virtual pump tech was gone. Instead, an elderly gentleman in a hospital gown shuffled over to sit on the tech's empty stool. The man's blue-rinsed hair blended oddly with the green shade of his skin, flaking off his face and neck in patches.

"It's me again, Dr. Oo. You couldn't resist operating, could you? Of course, it didn't particularly matter to me because I was almost dead when they brought me in from the Quintessence Mall. But you wouldn't let a fresh heart go to waste, so you opened me up anyway," the gentleman said.

"After surgery, they bagged me up, dead though with a new heart, and left me in the cold room. So, instead of cruising in my Bentley, I lay chilling and bloating, awaiting my ride across the river for cremation. I decidedly despised having my heart replaced with that of young Mr. Rao, just now resurrected from his ashes to join us. So, how about that, Oo?"

"This is nuts! This is some weird shit." Oo cried out. "It can't be happening."

"But it is happening, Oo," young Mr. Rao's voice resonated from his empty chest. "As to weird shit, we'll help you understand what weird really is." The virtual sound system delivered the cries of a keening wife and the wailing of three young children from afar.

Sanda vomited on the instrument table.

Oo slammed his instrument down. "Somebody turn the damned VR off! Turn the damn thing off!" He stomped on the foot pedal repeatedly. "Turn it off!" He ripped off his mesh cap, smashed it to the floor, and stomped on it.

Still gagging, Sanda said, "What were those things? Was that a hallucination like Hu warned us about?" She collapsed into a nearby chair. "At least they disappeared when I took off the VR cap."

However, for Dr. Oo, the figures with their stench of decay remained. "Sanda can't see us now, but you can," one of the bots said, "It's no hallucination, Oo. We'll be with you until your terrible debt is paid."

Overcome with fright and fury, Dr. Oo ripped away his surgical gown, swept the computers from their rack to the floor, flung the cameras against the wall, and fled the OR.

47. Vengeance

In the lab that afternoon, Dr. Hu mused, "I wonder how Oo's procedure is going. Ordinarily, I'd say our stratagem was cruel. What do you think, Angela? Julian? Wisut?"

"Not too cruel for Dr. Oo. I think he's a psychopath. To him, the ethnic minorities are subhuman, and he takes their hearts without a thought," Angela responded. "I hope our bots are driving him mad."

"I imagine they are," smiled Wisut. "Malcolm says such contrived hallucinations can persist, so they probably are taunting him."

Julian spoke succinctly, "I think he's addicted to yaba. I hope the zombie-bots keep him out of the operating room. That's no place for a psychopathic addict."

Just then, Hu's phone vibrated and scooted across the table. It was Dr. Oo, and he sounded beyond pissed. "I know it was you, you bastard, and I know why. I'll have your ass for this," Oo threatened. The call was dropped.

"He is enraged, panicky, scared shitless. No surprise," said Hu. "I think the apparitions are doing just what we'd hoped they would."

Later that night, Dr. Oo awakened, drenched in sweat and shivering. An evil smell hung in the air. "Maybe I'm having an epileptic olfactory aura. Maybe from a temporal lobe tumor that can be removed."

"Sorry, no tumor, Oo, that would be too easy. No, it's us. We're part of you now, embedded in your brain," came a Rohingya-accented voice. "Deny us if you like, but don't try to bargain. You stole our hearts, and we don't bargain. My English friend here had a diseased heart. Out it came and in went mine. In feats of incredible incompetence, you murdered us."

The Englishman sat in a chair by Oo's bed, moist from viscous fluids and sloughing bits of necrotic tissue.

"Yes, there's no way out, Oo. A neurosurgeon can't suck us out. Your astrologer can't help, and yaba makes us worse. We are part of you, and we can't be exorcised."

"How is this happening? Dr. Hu is messing with me." Enraged and hysterical, Dr. Oo gulped a yaba tablet and fled from his bed to the shower. He soaped and scrubbed and scrubbed. He dried off, polished his Teeth, gargled, spat, slathered on cologne, sprayed deodorant under his arms, and slicked his hair back. Finally, he fumbled through his bedside drawer and retrieved his colonial vintage 455 Webley top-break revolver. Oo inserted cartridges into the pistol and raced into the overcast night. "I told Hu I'd have his ass."

The banyan tree hovered ominously in the night sky, and its hairy roots seemed to reach out for Oo as he leaped into the SUV and sped sixteen kilometers down the empty highway to the airport. He roared up to the Otter's hanger and stumbled from the car to the ground. "Let me give you a hand," came a voice. Oo cried out as a slimy hand reached for him. He sprang to his feet, slid himself from the Rohingya's grip, and careened toward the plane.

The night attendant was aghast when he saw Dr. Oo heading for the general's Otter. The plane was already on loan and packed for a flight the next day. Moreover, heavy weather was upon them.

"Wait, Dr. Oo," the night attendant shouted. "It's instrument weather. You can't fly through it."

"Tell him what he can do to himself," Englishman said to Oo. "Who's he to tell you what you cannot do? Hop in. Go, go, go!"

Oo vaulted into the cabin, gulped a yaba, fired up the engines, taxied to the runway, and took off. A blinking tail light was the last thing seen of Dr. Oo as he powered the Otter into low-hanging clouds.

48. Bangkok Scimitar Report

Editors' Commentary: Here and Now

Today's front-page photo shows the billowing clouds and black smoke rising from the crash of a DHC-3 Otter whose flight originated in Naypyidaw, Burma. It was tracked by radar, flying erratically through a storm toward the Don Muang airport. The pilot, said to be Burma's only heart surgeon, had not filed a flight plan.

The authorities discovered a fortune in vibrant red rubies in the ashes of the smoking ruins. The Gemstone Lab has graded several as 'pigeon blood' rubies, the rarest and most beautiful, found only in extraordinary jewelry or museum exhibits. Several months ago, such an exhibit was stolen from the Rangoon Museum of the Arts. Precious stones, most particularly jade, from Burma are often termed 'genocide gemstones', referring to the fates of those who mine and smuggle them.

The values of various Burmese gems have exploded since the USA banned their international sales. The editors wonder if the authorities will discover purloined gems as they sift through the ashes of Dr. Oo's crash?

Investigators also found hundreds of black pebble-like bits that, on analysis, proved to be melted yaba. Given the erratic flight pattern, it is speculated that the pilot was flying under the influence of the drug. The cache of gems and yaba suggests that this doctor's income may not have depended entirely on surgery. A Webley top-break revolver was also recovered.

As ever, more to come!

As the weeks wore on, the *Bangkok Scimitar* continued to untangle the heart-on-ice deception. Readers ate it up. The Team Bangkok members were among them. The local Mafia members appreciated that the news shifted attention away from them and had laundered their reputations. Team Bangkok enjoyed a moment of great camaraderie.

Editors' Commentary: Here and Now

Following a raid on a newly renovated section of the formerly bankrupt Ratchathewi Hospital, local authorities took today's photo. The Bangkok police force descended on the hospital in response to a tip from a member of Bangkok's evolving Mafia. The hospital's renovated section was designed for cardiac surgery. The photo on the left shows a surgical suite containing anesthesia equipment, various monitors, and a heart-lung machine. The foggy image on the right was snapped inside the hospital's cold room.

The large bag on a bench within the cold room contained a decomposing body, currently under dental and DNA examination. Unfortunately, the body's grey-green tint was impossible to capture photographically through the haze. Not pictured are the immaculate patient rooms. The refinement of the renovated section sharply contrasts with the otherwise dilapidated condition of the hospital. Our Police Chier believes the illicit heart transplant operations were carried out in this operating suite, here in the heart of our city. The Scimitar's review of property transactions indicates that unidentified offshore investors purchased the bankrupt hospital for a token amount.

Our darkening skies have begun to clear for a new day in Bangkok. We thank our police for their sagacity, perseverance, and excellent work. We also tip our hats to the perceptive tipster who brought it all to light.

49. How the Big Boys Play

Boc and Khem flew again to Phnom Penh to bring Kimsan up to date and tie up loose ends.

Khem proceeded to tell Kimsan about how Nu Yee's encounter went down: how Yee had emerged from the cold room blue-lipped and scared shitless and confessed his role in the aberrant syndicate. So now, the Bangkok boss was in protective custody, soon to be with Interpol agents en route to Brussels.

"We ran Nu Yee's name by our Burma expert, Edna Cowling. Nu Yee is a bastard son of a General Wen Yee from the Wa province bordering China. Our Nu Yee is clever enough to work the Bangkok end of things but not enough to mastermind the syndicate. The mastermind has to be someone lots smarter, more connected, and certainly more prosperous—presumably General Wen Yee. Won't our triad friend Zhang find that interesting?

"Yes, and there's something else," Boc said. "The zombie-bot ruse apparently drove Dr. Oo nuts. Presumably seeking vengeance on Hu, Dr. Oo flew off into a rainstorm heading for Bangkok, crashed, and burned. Among the ashes, the authorities found a fortune in rubies and other gems. And the *Scimitar's* editors wonder if recently stolen pigeon blood rubies will be found among them. The trove of gems seems to validate Zhang's suspicion that the syndicate is smuggling more than hearts; that the hearts were a deception."

Khem added, "Yes, the team theorizes that someone in Burma saw the stars align and reasoned that falling kidney prices would make the idea of profitable heart transplant services credible. So, first recruit this jerk-off surgeon, Dr. Oo, as the goat. Then, distract the authorities by contriving a hit-and-run wreck to spill a heart in front of the syndicate's own photographer. Next, sell the photo to The *Bangkok Scimitar*, who would publish it. The photo would create a public hysteria that would force the authorities to shift their focus to finding a presumed heart syndicate. With the authorities distracted, the smugglers could haul in precious stones and whatever else at will.

"So, Team Bangkok's virtual-reality fake exposed Dr. Oo's role as the surgeon in the affair. However, Oo was not the prime mover, the brains and bucks behind the operation. The team also trapped the Bangkok boss, Nu Yee, and, with Edna Cowling's help, identified Nu's father, General Wen Yee, as the likely prime mover, the brains and great distractor. Zhang will appreciate the team's unraveling of these details. His Triad takes major offense when someone messes in their affairs."

"Milo always said the Burmese supply train 'snaked its way to Bangkok'. The team has amputated the tail in Bangkok, but they can't get to the head in Burma," said Boc.

"Very picturesque," said Kimsan. "The next step is to defang the snake. That goes beyond Team Bangkok's capabilities but not Zhang's or mine. Team Bangkok will need outside help."

"So I assume General Yee's position is not a desirable one," smiled Boc.

"To say the least, Khem. My associates and Zhang's triad will manage the Burma situation. Since General Wen Yee remains unaware of our knowledge, we can move deliberately."

Khem smiled, "Beware of fangs!"

Kimsan laughed.

50. Another Bangkok Scimitar Report

Editors' Commentary: Here and Now

Today's photo is of terrible destruction on such scale that virtually nothing remains to see. A major explosion occurred on a hillside beside Klong Haa, a canal on the west banks of the Chao Phraya river, leaving a broad patch of fractured concrete, smoking earth, and singed weeds. Neighborhood sources say the blast demolished a windowless brick building, occasionally visited by a black-and-orange long-tail boat. They say a sizeable amorphous bag was always heaved from the boat and taken into the demolished building.

Neighbors suspect that the building was an unlicensed crematorium, although none is listed at that site in the Bangkok Business Index. Perhaps a buildup of leaking gas caused the explosion, though questions remain. The Scimitar editors wonder if the crematorium might have borne some relationship to recent suspicions of illicit heart transplantation going on under our noses. You can be sure our investigative reporters are on it and will be reporting as things develop.

Editors' Extra: Here and Now

Just today, an anonymous source has informed the Scimitar that an Interpol officer took charge of a closely guarded Burmese prisoner, Nu Yee, for extradition to the Hague in association with the International Criminal Court's investigations of suspected genocide of ethnic people in Burma. Coincidentally Nu Yee's father, the prominent Tatmadaw General, Aung Wen Yee, and several associates disappeared while attending a golf invitational in the Wa province near the Chinese border.

51. Moving On

The team members relaxed at *Tii Baan* toward noon that day and reflected knowingly on the *Scimitar's* accounts of recent events. The 'heart-on-ice' matter was resolved, the general facts now public knowledge. The international opprobrium directed at Bangkok had diminished largely due to their efforts. The storm had passed.

Raising their glasses, the team toasted a mission accomplished, challenges met, dangers past, and allies with longer leashes than the UN had granted them. There was a touch of melancholy, for the team would likely enough dissolve and the members go their separate ways, just when they were having fun. So, they recounted the stories of their adventures over drinks, teased each other unmercifully, and promised to meet again. That would depend on a distant UN.

Toward midafternoon two men clad in black leather, Chinese, with prominent cheekbones and blue-black hair, entered *Tii Baan*. Smiling, they asked for Dr. Hu. Hu proffered a polite wai, introduced himself and welcomed them. "Won't you join us?"

The older of the two Chinese reciprocated formally but declined Hu's invitation. Then, reaching into his bag, he withdrew two meticulously wrapped packages and said, "Your Cambodian friend and our own leader hope you will accept these with their compliments as expressions of thanks and indebtedness. The leaders will remain at your service and hope someday to return the favor of your help."

"Thank you," began Hu. "But—" Before Hu could finish his sentence, the two men had mounted their motorcycles and were away, whirring down Soi Rangnam.

Hu opened the smaller package first. It contained a pair of miniature jadeite figurines of the Wat Phra guardian giants. A faceted pigeon-blood red ruby embedded in each giant's chest appeared to flicker whenever the light changed.

The second package contained black T-shirts with the image of a guardian giant sketched in gold paint on the front. Across the back, the words 'Imagination and Disruption' were stenciled in Thai script.

"Formidable as the Temple Guardians are we, huh?" The team members were totally pleased. They put the T-shirts on and toasted their new friends and benefactors.

As the afternoon wore on and conversations faded, Angela and Milo took a table by the sidewalk to watch ordinary people busying themselves along Soi Rangnam. "I'm happy to be in our shoes," said Milo.

Across Soi Rangnam, a fussy tour guide carrying a flag emblazoned with the RFC logo watched her tourist group swarm the fruit cart for iced mango, pineapple, and watermelon skewers and papaya, perfect for this hot day.

Angela noticed a middle-aged tourist detach himself from the group and start across Soi Rangnam toward *Tii Baan*. This Western *farang* wore safari shorts, black mid-calf socks and sandals, a yellow sleeveless T-shirt, black tiger-tooth neck glam, mirrored sunglasses, and an Aussie hat. A fanny pack rode his hip, and a backpack hung low behind him. He was grinning hugely. A sweet young thing clung to his arm.

"My God!" declared Angela smiling, "a Western tourist, straight from central casting right down to the 'lost chicken' on his arm. Perfect!" Stifling a giggle, she turned to point him out to Milo, who was already on his feet and grinning.

Laughing aloud, Milo hooted, "Why hello, Mr. Smith, you old chameleon—long time, no see. Your best disguise ever, down to the young lady on your arm!"

"Hi Milo," said Mr. Smith. "It's been, what, fifteen years, give or take? And, Angela, You've grown up to be a carbon copy of your mother plus a few shades of your dad's Thai. Hi Angela!"

Angela flashed back to the younger Mr. Smith, who had remembered her birthday with the set of Russian nesting dolls.

Milo chuckled, "Won't your tour group miss you and your, uh, companion?"

"Angela, Milo, meet my granddaughter, Kim. She's honored me with an hour of her busy university life. The group won't miss us. We just blended in."

"*Sawatdii Kha*," Kim waied and smiled. "My grandfather has told me so much about you. I can't wait to hear the old stories yet again. Sorry, but I've got to run to class now." She waied and was gone.

Mr. Smith accepted a bottle of Singha, smiled at Angela, sat, and opened his backpack. "Milo, get this package to Dow right away. It's vaccines; they need to stay cold until she immunizes the team. This folder here contains a new contract for Team Bangkok. They've lengthened your leash impressively." Mr. Smith drained his beer, set the bottle affirmatively on the tabletop, and asked directions to the WC.

Shortly, Mr. Smith emerged wearing skinny jeans, an Adidas T-shirt, a ball cap, and running shoes. "Milo, Angela, remember your past is never really past. Think hard about the contract. I'll show back up in a few days," he said and strolled toward the Skytrain station and was gone.

Angela and Milo felt the intoxication of imminent challenge.

Time for another doll to leave the nest, Angela thought, watching Milo slide a sheaf of documents out of the envelope. Finally, he gave a low whistle.

"This is gonna be good," he said.

The End

Acknowledgments

Thanks first to my wife, the protagonist in the story behind the story of Team Bangkok—Judy, who always keeps her bags packed, who at our retirement signed us up as adult learners with *Semester at Sea* for the voyage of a lifetime that eventually morphed into our years in SE Asia.

Almost twenty years later, events of those days endure and wear mature faces in the novel *Team Bangkok*. For example, Burma and Suu Kyi, Vietnam, Pol Pot's Khmer Rouge, China's belt-and-road initiative, transnational organized crime, (transplant tourism, drug and gem smuggling), western medicine vs. shamanic magic, layers of good and evil, artificial intelligence, and virtual reality are woven into the story.

Countless memories were shaken like dice, cast upon my imagination, and assembled into the reality of *Team Bangkok*. My thanks to Anne Larsen, wonderful teacher and editor, who helped me sort and shape this cluster of recollections.

Thanks to friends from the Soi Rangnam days in Bangkok. You know who you are; we drank plenty of beer together in Yim and Doug's restaurant. Thanks to Karen L. Click, Thailand English teacher, Voravut and Rnagsarn Chanyavanich, Bangkok natives, for cultural sensitivity readings and Sutthida and Aurarat for subtitle translation. To Judy Denton, Olivia Lucas, William McCann, and Ellen Hesse who proofed the novel, and Rena Pederson, author of *The Burma Spring,* for reading the *Edna Cowling* chapter. Also, thanks to Jim Latham, who recounts listening to enemy radio exchanges in Vietnam. Robert Hudgins, M.D. for comments on the ethics of transplant tourism, and Hugh Terrill for chit-chat about kidney transplant tourism at California cocktail parties. And to Surachai Sittijinda, our boss, head of the English Track in the Khon Kaen Wittayayon school where Judy and I taught. He revealed much of Thailand's culture to us.

Thanks also to the neurosurgeons in Thailand who shared their time with me: Voravut Chanyavanich, Chaiwit Thanapaisal, Amnat

Kithuandii, Thanat Vaniyapong, and Wanarak Watcharasaksilp, whom I met through the FIENS volunteer program of the American Association of Neurosurgeons.

Cover Design by FionaJaydeMedia.com

Author's Note

I. C. Denton, Jr., a retired neurosurgeon, and Judith Denton, a retired NASA engineer, fulfilled a life-long dream in the early 2000s when they moved to Thailand to learn more about Southeast Asia. They lived there for three years, one of which they spent teaching science and math in the English track in a public high school in Khon Kaen. They admire the Thai people, their rich culture, history, cuisine, and arts. This made Bangkok the perfect setting for Ira's first novel a medical thriller set in a complex city with a cast of Thai and American characters.

About the Author

I. C. Denton, Jr., a retired MD, and Judith Denton, a retired NASA engineer, fulfilled a life-long dream in the early 2000s when they moved to Thailand to learn more about Southeast Asia. They lived there for three years, one of which they spent teaching science and math in the English track in a public high school in Khon Kaen. They admire the Thai people and appreciate their rich culture, history, cuisine, and arts. Their experiences made Bangkok the perfect setting for Ira's first novel, a medical thriller set in a complex city with a cast of Thai and American characters